Gobbi Bonjour

and Other Short Stories

Paul Cotterell

To my fabulous family Jill, Abby and Nick

Properly wonderful people

(I may be a little biased!)

With special thanks to Chris Sutton, whose excellent stories inspired me to write these.

Contents

Crosstown Traffic

"Good man!" said Alan to himself as he drove towards the random man waving on the grass verge beside the dual carriageway. Dressed in a yellow hi-vis jacket, grey track suit and matching bobble hat, he was waving to encourage drivers to slow down before they reached a mobile police speed trap further down the road. Alan wasn't a habitual speeder but he was grateful for the warning as the 40mph speed limit was, in his opinion, unrealistic for this large open road and it was easy to creep over it. He waved an acknowledgement to the young man who nodded and continued making large, deliberate "slow-down" movements with his hands to the drivers behind Alan.

It was a sunny, crisp winter afternoon and the white police van was clearly visible up ahead. Alan cruised past at 35, thinking it best not to wave, grateful not to have been caught.

"Where are you on Saturday night when there's trouble in town?!" he thought, slightly annoyed as he approached the town. He appreciated the need for road safety but, in *that* place? At *that* time? "Not exactly a priority!" he thought.

Alan picked up some supplies in town and headed home an hour later. As he came back over the brow of the hill, he noticed the police van was still there on the other side of the carriageway and bobble hat boy was still there too!

"Must be freezing" Alan thought to himself, "although he's keeping active!" It was then that he realised that there was a clear line of sight between the young man and the Police van . . .

"What!? Why would the Police tolerate that?! Got to be reducing his catch rate . . . probably perverting the course of justice too!" thought Alan as he passed the animated young man.

At home, as he poured milk into his mug of coffee, the incident circled in his mind.

"Maybe he's just part of a road safety package" he thought "as long as people slow down, that's the important thing".

"Never seen him" said Viv behind the bar of the Moon & Stars, pouring Alan's pint.

"I don't understand it" said Alan "Bold as brass in a hi-vis vest! Camouflage would have been more understandable!"

"Might be because of that accident" said Viv reaching for crisps.

"Oh, what was that?" asked Alan

"Last month . . . teenager ran into the dual carriageway, driver didn't have a chance apparently"

"Dear God . . . no I didn't hear that" said Alan concerned.

"It was in the Echo"

"Shamefully, I don't often read it" said Alan

"Didn't see any flowers or such, either" added Alan.

"She wasn't local. Pretty mind. Blonde girl about 14 she was. Never know when your time's up do you" she said smiling, taking the last of the wind out of Alan's sails before turning to serve the next customer.

Alan wandered home, a short, crisp walk under a clear velvet sky, Venus sitting bright and high. "That Echo's probably still in the recycling" he thought.

He sorted through the pile of papers in the wicker basket in his porch and there it was . . . front page news. *Teenager killed* read the stark headline.

And there she was, looking out of the paper at Alan, pretty as Viv had said, and happy, as those photos always seemed to be. It was just as Viv had described, Amanda apparently stepping into the road to catch a plastic bag she had dropped, the driver having no time to react. Neither were local, Amanda visiting her cousin and the driver just passing through.

"All for a bloody plastic bag" he thought, the melancholy of the evening tiring him enough to decide on an early night.

Alan always dreamed more after a drink but that night was unusual, even by his standards. He dreamt that he answered the front door to find Amanda standing bolt upright, expressionless. As he went to speak, she smiled and giggled, eyes full of life and ran off. He then settled back to watching TV when the door bell rang again. It was Amanda again, who again ran off laughing as soon as he tried to talk. The dream played on a loop like a stuck record until he woke, his unsettled sleep only adding to his tiredness.

Bleary-eyed he rushed down a bowl of cereal and jumped into his car to head for work. The petrol light blinked empty at him.

Damn!" he thought, already late and realising he wouldn't make it without a stop.

He hurried down the dual carriageway towards the nearest garage, the wind buffeting his car. And there he was again! Bobble hat boy in his grey track suit and hi-vis!

"Jesus, he's on the early shift this morning!" Alan thought, the boy still boldly gesticulating to passing motorists.

After hurriedly half-filling his tank, he swung onto the roundabout and joined the dual carriageway heading back, picking up speed.

"I'm late now . . . not much point in rushing" he thought.

It happened so quickly . . . the girl ran out from nowhere. The wind had caught her frog umbrella and blown it straight in front of Alan's car, the young girl darting after it instinctively. Alan's legs instantly straightened, hitting the brake and clutch together as his arms braced against the steering wheel. His eyes were fixed on the girl as his car squealed to a stop, the girl frozen in shock in front of his bonnet.

Loosening his grip on the wheel, Alan jumped out of the car.

"Are you OK?!" he said shaking, ushering the girl onto the grass verge, her face puckering up, starting to cry.

"What were you *thinking*!?" shouted her father running across to her.

"I'm sorry" said the young girl through her tears.

Her father scooped her up.

"Thank God . . . .thank God" he kept saying as he cuddled his daughter.

"Thank you" he said looking to Alan.

Alan raised his hand to him and smiled, pleased he had reacted quickly enough. As he walked back to his car, the bobble hat boy stood in front of him holding the frog umbrella. Smiling, he passed it to Alan.

"Thank you" Alan said, taking the umbrella.

He turned back to the father and daughter.

"There you go" he said passing the umbrella to the girl. Her red face lit up.

"What do you say, Jenny" said her father.

"Thank you" she beamed.

"You should thank that man over there" said Alan, pointing back to the bobble hat boy.

"What man?" said the girl, wiping her eyes.

With a smile for Alan, the bobble hat boy took off his hat with one hand. Long blonde hair tumbled out and Amanda waved a goodbye, still smiling. Her work was done and, like a dandelion clock, the wind blew her away, grey dust snaking across the surface of the road.

Giant

What's that in the field? asked Freddie, pointing out of the car window.

"Ah, that's a giant's armchair that is" said his father playfully.

George enjoyed the drive through the villages to Freddie's pre-school and it was glorious this sunny morning, just open green fields, tree-lined hedgerows and blue skies. And on its own, in the middle of a large green field, Freddie had spotted a haystack, for all the world looking like a huge comfortable armchair.

"Giant's armchair?! There's no such thing as giants!" said Freddie smiling.

"*No such thing as giants!*" exclaimed his father "If that's the case, why would there be one of their chairs in the field then?!"

Being a father suited George and he loved Freddie's wide-eyed innocence.

The weather held for the next day and, as they passed the same field, Freddie pointed out excitedly "There's the giant's chair again!"

"Of course" said his father with a wry smile "they need somewhere to rest after a hard day's work, don't they"

"Are you *sure* Daddy?! I think you're telling fibs! Mummy says you're telling fibs"

"Ah, *does* she . . ." smiled his father "Well, I'm afraid mummy can't see them because she's a girl"

"*Really?*"

"Yes, it's only boys who can see giants" said his father seriously "What do they teach you at that school?!"

"Ha, ha!" chuckled Freddie "I can't see any giants . . ." he said looking hard across the wide green fields.

"Well, you *won't* during the *day*. They come out late in the evening after you've gone to bed"

"*Really?*" smiled Freddie.

"Of course! That's why if you ask your friends if they've seen one, I don't think they will have because they're only out late"

Freddie sounded a little concerned.

"Are they *good* giants?"

Sensing he may have planted a seed of worry, George reassured his son, "Of course they are! There's no such thing as a bad giant! They're *all* good. Every one I've met has been very kind"

"That's good" replied Freddie relieved.

"It is!" agreed his father.

After a little thought Freddie asked his father "When did you see one?"

"I suppose I was about your age when I first saw one" smiled his father "All very friendly though, quite shy actually"

"I think *I'd* like to see one" smiled Freddie.

"Perhaps we'll go out for a walk when you're a bit older and try and find one. What do you think?"

"Yeeeeess!" shouted Freddie.

"They're hard to find mind. Very shy"

The following day, two more large haystacks had appeared in the field.

"There's more chairs!" Freddie shouted.

"Yes, it looks like he's had some friends round doesn't it"

"More giants?" asked Freddie.

"I think so, or they wouldn't have had the extra furniture delivered . . . you know that furniture advert you like? . . ."

"*Furniture World!*" Freddie shouted. He knew the song in the advert off by heart.

"That's it. Well, they make big stuff for giants too. But they have to make them out of hay because people would wonder what was going on if there were big flowery sofas in the middle of a field"

"*Really?*" said Freddie, doubtfully.

Yes, *really*" his father teased "they can all sit down and have a chat and a bucket of tea"

"A bucket!" Freddie giggled. He liked the idea of that.

"*You're* a giant!" Freddie shouted at his father.

"Well I *am* quite tall but real giants are *really* big!"

"Stop it!" giggled Freddie.

"They're *so* tall they just pluck birds out of the sky and eat them for snacks!"

This really caught Freddie off guard and he burst into uncontrollable giggling.

"Arrrrgh!" he shouted, his fingers in his ears, trying to shut his Dad out, sniffing bubbles up his nose.

"Stop it. I'll tell Mummy!"

Later that night, just after the sun had gone down, George walked across the fields to see them. It had been a long time.

He had always seen them as a child, normally at night, and soon he would bring Freddie down to show him, like *his* father had done.

There were three in the middle of the field, relaxing quietly on their chairs.

Of course, George had been joking about Furniture World, they had made them themselves.

Love is the Sweetest Thing

"You are *kidding* me!" said Lucy almost choking on her coffee.

"No, it's Connor!" assured Kate.

"Oh, I'm not sure about that" said Lucy uneasily, pulling Kate's hand closer "Let me have a closer look".

The diamond was a pale yellow set in a gold ring. "Wow...how much was *that*?" said Lucy, thinking it somehow looked cheaper than it probably was.

"You don't want to know" replied Kate.

"Oh I do!" Lucy said.

"Two and a half thousand"

"Wow!" said Lucy again. "Two and half thousand to have your husband on your finger"

Four months ago, Kate had lost her husband to Motor Neurone Disease, a particularly cruel condition that can take different forms but, for Connor, it was a slow, undignified deterioration. He gradually lost control of muscle movement from the feet upwards, a relentless debilitation creeping up his body...couldn't walk, couldn't control bowel movements, couldn't make love, couldn't sit up, couldn't breathe … When the end came, Kate honestly saw it as a happy release.

"Yes, it's expensive, but when you consider it is actually *him*, it's pretty cool isn't it" said Kate.

She had read about the company in a magazine. "Life's Jewel" could create a diamond from Connors' ashes, reprocessing the carbon to create a ring … "a lasting momento". "Each stone is unique" the advert read, "with its own character … just like your loved one … you can share those special moments again …" The description was cheesy but the concept, captured Kate's imagination.

"Correct me if I'm wrong" said Lucy "but you weren't that close were you?!"

"No!" laughed Kate "that's true enough!"

Kate really did see Connor's death as a happy release … for both of them.

The day after his death, she couldn't stop smiling. She knew it looked bad but she couldn't help it. Living through his slow deterioration, caring for him the last few months had been a difficult time. People expecting to see the loving, grieving wife … but she remembered the evenings she spent on her own while he was "at work", the affairs … There was even a time when she felt he deserved it for what he'd done. She felt guilty for that but, when the end came, there was little love left.

"So why did you have it made?" asked Lucy.

"I don't know. I saw the advert and thought it was bit quirky". It certainly wasn't any sense of Kate wanting Connor always by her side. She had got used to him not being there long ago.

Not long before Connor's diagnosis, she had seen other men. "If you can't beat them, join them" she thought. The dating agencies hadn't been entirely successful in their selections, throwing up some truly undesirables, although it *did* give her some stories to tell her friends:

"Body odour just didn't cover what he smelt like!"

"He was on the phone to his mother longer than he talked to me!"

Even the more desirables soon became a problem when they realised Kate was quite a wealthy woman. It seemed to bring out the worst.

She'd even tried some of the more exclusive services, the one's that only trade in well-heeled executives. They *did* smell much better, but they didn't really do it for her. "There's no money in poetry and no poetry in money" Kate remembered someone famous had once said and, for her, that had proven to be true.

A series of one-night stands filled a need to prove to herself that she still "had it" but after a while, the whole business nibbled away at the soul.

And Kate hadn't taken her new ring off once. She didn't wear it on her wedding ring finger but on the middle, making her availability clear. And there Connor sat . . . through all the internet searches and the awkward fumbling.

She would fiddle with it while she sat watching TV. It had become quite a habit, twiddling and turning the ring subconsciously.

"Leave it alone" Lucy would say at their coffee mornings, "you'll make him dizzy!" But somehow it felt comforting.

Lately she had noticed that the ring was becoming a bit more difficult to move, a little tighter than it had been.

This didn't make any sense as, over the last few months, Kate had tried hard to get into shape before hitting the dating circuit.

"Got to make an effort" she'd say to Lucy. And she *had*, losing three stone and treating herself to a whole new wardrobe. All the way through her weight loss, the ring had always felt comfortable, never loose, which she found strange as she was definitely slimmer. Strangely, it was as if the ring was shrinking with her! Recently, Kate had stopped losing weight but the ring had started to tighten a little, to the point where her absent minded twiddling became difficult. To start, she thought nothing of it but then it became harder to ignore. She tried to take it off but there was no way it was coming over her knuckle, the ring now looking much too small. Over the next few days her finger started to ache and her knuckle swelled until, one night, the pain kept her awake. Turning on her pillow she thought "Paracetamol's not touching it . . . doctors tomorrow".

"Kate Burnham, Room 2" announced the tannoy in the waiting room.

She'd arrived early as an "emergency appointment" and it was pot luck which doctor she'd get, but she'd been lucky.

"Ooh, Dr. Shimame" she thought, smiling for the first time that morning.

He was always a bonus for Kate. Although traditional in his suit, she could easily imagine his chiselled Arabian looks draped in white robes, effortlessly pulling her onto the back of his horse, galloping across the desert. Despite her thinly veiled flirting on previous appointments, Dr.Shimame maintained a professional distance, smiling, adorable.

"And how can I help you today, Mrs Burnham?"

Thinking of several different ways Dr. Shimame could "help", Kate resisted sharing them with him, coughed and said "It's this ring Doctor", raising her hand.

"Ah yes, I can see" he said holding her hand. Kate's heart fluttered slightly.

"That's not good. Have you hit it?"

"No, it's just getting tighter, I don't really understand it"

"Mmm . . . must be some local inflammation, maybe an infection" he said under his breath, looking more closely for signs of cuts or abrasion.

"Nothing obvious here . . . you may have knocked it without noticing" he said.

"I haven't" said Kate, knowing full well that she hadn't, "the ring's just been getting smaller for some reason. It's odd, you'd expect it to get looser if anything . . . with wear"

Dr. Shimame looked at her with his deep brown eyes and decided he didn't have time to get into a debate about shrinking jewellery.

"We'll get you on some antibiotics, but this ring will have to come off now I'm afraid"

"That's fine, just take it off" Kate replied, grateful for some relief on the horizon.

"I'm sorry but I'll have to cut it off, there's no other way"

"That's fine" smiled Kate "I'll get it repaired"

Dr Shimame slipped the blade of the snips under the tight ring and in a single snip, cut through the soft gold.

It immediately felt more comfortable "Ahh, that's better"

"Move your fingers for me" said Dr Shimame.

Kate obediently wiggled.

"All seems good. We'll get you on those antibiotics and I don't think you'll have too much . . . " He hesitated and rubbed the back of her hand.

"Has this mole always been here?" he asked.

"I don't know . . . yes, I think so"

"I think we'll get this one checked out" said Dr Shimame with the minimum of drama.

"Do you think there's a problem then?" asked Kate.

"Probably not, but I like to be on the safe side. We'll get the dermatologist to have a look at it"

"Not only a dreamboat, but a bloody good doctor" said Kate to Lucy sipping her coffee in the kitchen.

"Was there a problem then?" enquired Lucy.

"Yes, it was a melanoma, skin cancer ... if it wasn't for Dr. Shimame I could have been in real trouble"

"If it wasn't for that ring tightening you mean" replied Lucy "why would it do that?"

"I don't know" said Kate looking directly at Lucy "I can't figure it out. The jewellers said I'm about two ring sizes smaller now. *You* know I was losing weight ..." Lost in thought, Lucy twiddled her repaired ring around her finger, a perfect fit now.

"I've been thinking" said Lucy seriously, "it's almost like Connor was looking out for you".

Kate looked up at Lucy. And it was then it happened ... a well of memories bubbled up through her ... of happier times when her and Connor had first met, living by the coast ... when they were in love.

In that moment, Kate finally realised what her and Connor had lost. And she cried.

The Tunnel

"Can you do the business again, Joe?" asked Dan.

"You love it don't you" replied Joe smiling, "sending me down there, the resident canary!"

Joe didn't have to go down the tunnels often, maybe once a month, but it was part of his job, testing the air for the maintenance team, making sure it was breathable and there was no build-up of dangerous gases.

"I should dress up in a yellow bird suit for you!" said Joe to Dan the engineer.

"I'd like that!" joked Dan.

The job *was* like a human canary . . . to test the air from the manhole entrance, a tube would be dangled into the space to sample the air with electronic gas monitors before going down there. If it was safe and the monitors didn't alarm, Joe would climb down the metal ladder into the tunnel, monitors slung over both shoulders like school satchels, and walk to the work area to see if there were any problems. One monitor was checking for oxygen levels, one for flammable gas, and they were both set to alarm way before there was a problem, giving him a chance to get out. He knew that any problem was very unlikely. The tunnel was lined in grey concrete and very clean, if a little dusty and the maintenance team would normally lift a few manholes to get some air circulating. The only potential problems were leaks from the piped gas services that ran through the tunnels, which was unlikely as the tunnels were fairly new and well-maintained.

"One of these days I'm going to trip in here and it'll be Christmas before you buggers notice I'm gone!" said Joe as he pulled the sampling tube up from the manhole.

Dan laughed. "As I'm writing out your Christmas card, I'll be thinking: Mmm . . . *Joe?* I haven't seen him for *weeks* . . . and you can't miss him in that bird suit!"

They would never do the tunnel work alone, always two or more people but, for some reason, Joe did the gas tests on his own, albeit with an engineer standing by at the entrance.

"I'm going in!" said Joe, squawking like a bird and flapping his arms "Have my seed ready for when I get back!"

"See you soon" laughed Dan.

Joe climbed down the wall ladder, stepped on to the smooth concrete floor of the tunnel and flicked on the lights. That was always amazing. On came the fluorescent light tubes along the ceiling of the tunnel, each lighting up in turn as the light spread down the long tunnel's seemingly endless length.

Of course it *did* end, at a corner, when another long stretch would reveal itself. The tunnel was smooth, grey concrete on the walls, floor and ceiling with pipes running along both walls, all very clean and modern, the opposite to a war-time escape tunnel, no mud anywhere. Clinical even. And Joe had never seen a rat or any other animal down there, not even a big spider, which surprised him as there was half a mile of tunnels and he thought he'd have seen something by now.

Joe checked the monitors were on and started to walk, his footsteps echoing. The tunnel was quite large being about as tall and wide as an average living room and, being brightly lit, it wasn't too claustrophobic for him. But it could get disorientating down there, everything looking the same . . . grey walls, lights, pipes and very little else and sometimes, as he walked deeper into the tunnel system, his imagination got the better of him.

"I'm the only thing down here" he'd start to think.

"What if the lights fail?" He knew there was a generator but he'd watched too many horror films . . . lights failing, a moan at the end of the corridor, psychopathic patients in blood-stained gowns wandering hospital basements . . .

"You all right Joe? Over." Dan's voice on the radio was well-timed to break the tension.

"Yes. Arrrkk!" smiled Joe, impersonating a canary and pleased to hear his voice.

Dan sniggered, "Good. Speak in a few minutes. Out"

Joe had an unusually long walk today, a little deeper into the tunnel than usual, a round trip of around thirty minutes.

He turned the first corner at the end of the long stretch and was faced with the same view that was around *every* corner down there . . . another long, arrow-straight row of lights disappearing into the distance.

On longer walks, he would play some music out loud through his phone to distract himself from the isolation. The acoustics down there were good, producing a "surround-sound" effect.

"Shuffle" he said to himself as he tapped the screen, feeling lucky and the opening chords of The Jam's "Going Underground" abruptly broke the silence.

"What are the chances of that!" he smiled, nodding his head to the beat and humming along *"Going underground! Going underground . . . "* as he carried on down the grey tube.

Joe had come to the conclusion that it must have been cheaper to build the tunnels straight as there wasn't a curved section in sight.

"Some curves might break the boredom, though" he thought.

"Then again, at least you can see what's up there!" he added, allowing a slight insecurity to creep back.

Joe glanced at the monitors. No problems there. There never was.

Next up on the shuffle selection was a particular favourite of his: "Supermassive Black Hole" by Muse, again strangely appropriate, he thought.

"Oh *yes!*" said Joe out loud, the acoustics of the tunnel seeming to add to the song as he started to sing and dance. He found it impossible not to.

"Oh baby I'm a fool for no-one,
but ooo baby I'm a fool for you,
You've got me under false pretences . . . "

He spun around the tunnel, the monitors spreading like a chair-o-plane, lost in the song. Then suddenly, the music stopped, bringing his dance to an end, the chair-o-plane slowing as the monitors settled by his side.

He looked down . . . "Damn, out of charge!" he cursed, pressing buttons to no avail.

"Damn!"

He continued to walk into the tunnel, fiddling with his phone but there were no signs of life. As he looked up, he immediately walked into the end of a metal pipe support, hitting him square in the forehead. Joe fell to the floor with a clatter of monitors and radio and lay there unconscious, bleeding from the neat U-shaped cut in his forehead.

He wasn't out for long, only a few minutes.

"Erghh.." he groaned confused, slowly regaining consciousness. He sat up slowly, raising his hand to his forehead. It was wet and covered in blood, a little too much for Joe's comfort.

"Shit!" He looked down at the dark red pool on the floor, the only colour in the grey tunnel, save a few coloured stripes on the pipes to identify their contents.

"You idiot!" Joe said to himself, wiping his forehead with the sleeve of his black shirt, his black trousers covered in grey dust. He cleaned his face as best he could, and slowly got up on his feet. Some clarity returning, he looked down to the monitors and was relieved to find them both still working . . . they were expensive . . . then, head pounding, he looked down the tunnel at the lights leading off into the distance.

"Odd" he thought. Something was different. The lights didn't go so far and the tunnel looked for all the world like it curved to the left on a gentle arc. "Must be the knock" he thought, shutting his eyes and shaking his head.

But, as he stumbled down the tunnel, the view stayed the same, this constant, gentle curve.

The radio crackled on, "You alright down there Joe? Over"

Joe fumbled the radio from the carrier on his belt and pressed the button.

"Not really mate" replied Joe through the pain "I've taken a bit of knock on my head".

"Are you OK? Over" asked Dan concerned.

"Yes, yes" Joe replied "but I think I'll come out".

"Good idea. Can you make your way to an exit? Over"

"Can't see one, but I'll walk on a bit"

"I'll get someone to you if you need it, Joe. Over" said Dan.

"No, it's fine Dan, I'm OK. Over"

Joe walked further into the tunnel looking for position markings on the wall or any ladders or manholes on the ceiling. Nothing in view, so he walked on . . .

The view stayed the same, his whole world, grey and gently curving to the left.

"What the hell *is* this!" Joe said to himself. He leaned against the pipes along the wall to try to clear his head but it made no difference.

"Any luck Joe? Over" said Dan.

"Not yet . . ." replied Joe "are there any curved sections of tunnel down here, I don't know about? Over"

"What?"

"Any parts that aren't straight that you know about . . . because that's what I'm in"

"You *know* it's all straight . . . are you sure you're OK?"

"I'm telling you, it's not straight down here!" replied Joe adamantly.

"Look Joe, we'll get someone down to you"

"OK, maybe you should" replied Joe, a little lost.

"Leave it with me—I'll get some back-up and come down to you myself. Over"

In a few minutes, Dan had organised a colleague to stand by on the surface, and he climbed down the same ladder into the tunnel that Joe had descended on earlier.

"I'm down here now, Joe. Can you tell me where you are at the moment? Any position markers on the walls? Over"

"No I can't! I've been walking since we spoke and there's nothing" replied Joe, a slight tremor in his voice.

"Must be something, mate" replied Dan, not wanting to state the obvious. "It's marked every ten metres remember, on both walls? Over"

"I know where it's bloody marked, it's just not there!"

"OK, mate, OK. Try to keep calm, I'm on my way to you."

Joe kept walking and the tunnel kept curving to the left. He started jogging, easy for Joe as outside the tunnel he would regularly run 5k. But there was still no change. Catching his breath, he radioed Dan.

"Dan. It's me. Over"

"Go ahead mate. Where are you?"

"I'm in trouble Dan. Everything's the same down here. I've gone another kilometre and nothing's changed ... must have wandered into a part of the tunnel we're not aware of. Over"

Dan knew that every inch of those tunnels was known, every pipe, sign and man-hole down there was documented.

"Don't worry mate. I'm making my way towards you now, shouldn't be long"

"I'm losing charge on the radio" said Joe "Only one bar left." It would normally have been fully charged in its holder but he'd grabbed this one from the bench in a hurry earlier.

"OK mate, save it and I'll get back to you soon. Out"

Joe carried on jogging, another two kilometres at least, but there was no change at all. Dan continued to quickly search the long straight tunnels, until he came to the last stretch.

"Joe, it's me" said Dan.

"Receiving. Where are you?" asked Joe.

"More to the point, where are *you!* I've walked all the tunnels and I'm looking down the last stretch now" said Dan curtly "If you're pissing about I'll bloody kill you!"

With that, the green light on Joe's radio stopped blinking. He was out of charge.

"Damn!" Joe checked his phone. A bar of charge left but no reception ... he knew it was a black spot.

Head still hurting, Joe continued to bear left on his walk. As both monitors beeped to indicate they needed charging he shivered, the temperature in the tunnel consistently cool.

Hazel, Joe's girlfriend, had arrived at the site at half 5 to pick Joe up, as usual.

"He's still in the tunnel finishing off" explained Dan in a white lie "he shouldn't be too long" and left her to wait in reception with a cup of coffee.

"What do I tell her?" he thought. His team had searched everywhere, and checked everywhere again and still they couldn't find him. He'd repeatedly tried to contact Joe on the radio, but all he heard was a crackly silence.

For Joe, the tunnel stayed the same ... grey walls, pipes ... clean, if a little dusty. No spiders, no rats ... no food at all ... and no water.

Joe had tried shouting, so much his throat hurt and he was tired of the echo of his voice. For the first two days, he'd tried hitting the pipework with the metal case of a monitor. It was loud and he would hit them for hours, hoping that the pipes would carry the noise to the surface and someone would hear him. But there was no response.

He couldn't sleep, the bright lights were on all the time . . . so he carried on walking, looking for signs, wall-markings, man-holes . . . but there were none. On the third day, cold and thirsty, Joe noticed a dark mark on the floor up ahead that he hadn't seen before . . .

"A hatch . . . a drain!" he thought excitedly running towards it. But when he got closer, his heart sank . . . it was the stain of his blood on the floor from his accident. Joe had walked in a circle.

"In a straight tunnel, I've walked in a big circle!" he thought, unable to stop a desperate smile crossing his face.

He lost count of the times he walked the circle over the next few days, always ending up at the blood-stained floor. In the end, Joe settled on that spot. Unable to think clearly, tired and cold, he felt more comfortable there, laying down quietly on the floor, the stain a touchstone to the way his life used to be.

And then the lights went out.

Simon

The pig caught Jack's eye as soon as he walked into the village hall. How could it not! Perched majestically on the table, about a quarter of the size of the real thing with big black eyes, the not-unrealistic furry toy pig overlooked the rest of the bric-a-brac, with the air of a lion looking over its pride.

Jack smiled at Jessica, his friend's daughter who was running the stall.

"Now *that* is a fine pig!" he said.

"You're joking! It's so ugly!" she replied.

"Ugly! He's a thing of beauty" joked Jack, while genuinely being quite taken with it.

"I can see he needs a good home. I'll give you £7, if you take him off the table now and put him aside for me"

"No way!" she laughed "I can't take £7 for that! Give me three and he's yours"

"Deal!" smiled Jack, reaching for the coins in his wallet.

"An absolute bargain!"

Jessica passed the pig to Jack who pretended to cradle it in his arms and stroke its head. She was starting to worry about him now.

"He's a lot lighter than I thought!" said Jack.

Jack lived in a fairly modest house in the village, modest compared to some of the houses. After twenty years running his business, he'd just paid off the mortgage and with Michelle, his eldest, at University and Elise his youngest at work, this meant more time with his wife, Jen. Life had come full circle for them. They were married thirteen years before having children and enjoyed every day, and now, as much as they loved their children, they were enjoying getting that time back.

"What the hell is that!" shouted Elise as Jack walked into the hall, the pig under his arm.

"It's a pig" pointed out Jack "isn't he lovely!"

"Actually he is!" Elise smiled, stroking the soft pig-coloured fur on his head.

"He's got beautiful eyes" she said looking into its large black eyes.

"Where are you going to put that!" said Jen as she caught sight of Jack's new acquisition.

"I thought, the living room, he won't take up too much room"

"How much did you pay for him!" enquired Jen, having experienced some unusual purchases in the past.

"Only three of the Queen's pounds!" laughed Jack "where else can you get a fine ornamental pig for that money?"

"He *is* quite cute isn't he" said Jen stroking his head.

Jack positioned the pig in the corner of the living room and it instantly looked at home, looking across the room over his slightly wrinkled snout.

"Simon" Elise said randomly as they watched TV.

"What?" said Jack turning to her.

"Simon. That's his name" she said

"You're right you know!" agreed Jack "Simon it is!" Elise picked up Simon and positioned him between her and her Dad to watch TV.

Over the coming weeks, Simon really became part of the family, perched on people's lap's being absent-mindedly stroked and often used as a footstool.

Simon *was* a lot lighter than he looked, all his strength coming from a sturdy wire frame that could be felt through the fur at his shoulder blades.

Over time, Simon's initial novelty inevitably waned and he wasn't petted as often as when he first took up residence but he was always a feature of that corner of the room, always welcome.

"You might want to sit down" said Jen seriously to Jack.

"Why?" replied Jack, expecting bad news.

"Your brother and his nephew are on their way over now". This was said in the manner of lighting the blue touch-paper and standing well back.

"Oh great!" shouted Jack sarcastically. "What I have I done to deserve that?!" His nephew's visit always involved a damage limitation exercise where anything breakable had to be moved beyond his boisterous seven-year-old reach and a constant eye kept on him for violent lunges. Jack didn't blame Marty, he was young. He blamed his brother who just put his feet up, sipped a cup of tea and enjoyed the break!

"Ted! Good to see you!" welcomed Jack opening the door, almost sounding sincere.

Marty ran into the house between Jack's legs and the assault by Tasmanian Devil began.

"It could have been a lot worse …" Jack thought to himself, surveying the house after the visit. Only a broken photo-frame and some chocolate on the white carpet, mainly because Jack had distracted them with a game of football in the garden for most of the visit.

Later that day, Jack and Elise were relaxing in front of the TV.

"Where's Simon?" asked Elise, concerned he was missing from his normal corner.

"Don't know" replied her father quizzically "Seen Simon anywhere?" he shouted to Jen in the kitchen.

"I'm not his keeper!" she shouted back, "in the corner the last time I saw him".

Curious, Jack got up and had a look round the house and Simon was nowhere to be seen. Then a penny dropped …

"It's that bloody kid isn't it!"

"No, it wouldn't be" said Jen trying to calm him "although I haven't seen the pig since they've been …"

"I'm sorry" said Ted on the phone. "He sneaked the pig out in a bag when I wasn't looking"

"That would be most of the time!" thought Jack uncharitably.

"I'm afraid he's been riding it in the garden …"

"Oh great!" thought Jack.

" … and he managed to cut himself on a wire that stuck out"

"Well it's not really a toy!" said Jack, realising that it probably was.

"Anyway, some of the stuffing has come out and we're having it properly repaired for you. Hope that's OK"

"OK. Thanks. That's fine" said Jack resigned "thanks for letting us know".

"Did you tell him?" asked Rosemary, Ted's wife.

"No" replied Ted smiling "he didn't mention anything so it can't be theirs can it!" Ted was talking about some of the stuffing that came out of Simon. Most of it was conventional, but some if it definitely was not. Nestled in the centre of the pig, Ted had found a plastic bag containing some bank notes, forty thousand dollars to be precise. Four hundred, $100 dollar bills wrapped in plastic film!

"If it was *his* money, he'd have made a fuss!" said Ted.

"I bet it's the Columbian connection then" said Rosemary, smiling, "I can't believe it!" Rosemary had noticed a small Columbian label underneath Simon and, although it sounded a bit fanciful, she suspected that it was probably drugs related, possibly a way of getting money out of the country in a child's toy? Whether this was the truth or not, neither Ted nor Rosemary saw the need to complicate the situation by mentioning their discovery to Jack.

"We can get that car now!" said Rosemary excited.

"We've repaired that pig!" said Ted over the phone to Jack, "good as new now, probably better . . . they've put some material over the wire inside so it doesn't poke out again".

"OK" said Jack unimpressed.

"Do you want me to drop him off?" asked Ted.

"Unusually helpful of him" Jack thought.

"I'll have something to show you" said Ted.

"Oh? What's that?" asked Jack, failing to disguise his disinterest.

"You'll have to wait and see."

Jack opened the door to his brother, holding the pig.

"What do you think?!" said Ted, handing him the repaired pig and stepping aside so Jack could see the BMW convertible on the drive.

"Very nice!" said Jack politely, not convinced by the garish green.

"Yeah, we had a bit of luck on the lottery last week—10K!" said Ted, underselling their windfall.

"Congratulations" Jack replied weakly, finding it difficult to muster the false enthusiasm.

"Rosemary always wanted one, so we thought, why not?! Life's too short!"

"Can be" said Jack.

"Anyway, we wanted to share our good luck, so here's a little something for you and Jen" smiled Ted handing Jack an envelope.

"No, we couldn't possibly acc-"

"We won't hear of it" interrupted Ted, "We both want to. We'll be offended if you say no!"

Jack looked at the envelope. He really didn't want a hand-out from his brother. "It's five hundred pounds" said Ted beaming "treat yourselves on us"

It was the last thing Jack wanted but, as Ted was persistent, he decided on a grateful acceptance rather than an argument.

"Well, that's fantastic Ted. Thank you so much. And please thank Rosemary for us. It's very kind"

"Least we can do" said Ted, as he turned back to his car. He rarely stayed long enough to say anything meaningful.

Slightly dazed, Jack walked back into the house, Simon under his arm.

"You are not going to believe what's just happened!" Jack told Jen, clutching the envelope.

"Surprise me" smiled Jen.

"Ted and Rosemary have just given us five hundred quid!"

"What!" said Jen "you're joking! What's the catch?"

"I know, there *must* be one, but it was a lottery win and he insisted" replied Jack still bemused.

"Bloody hell! Well, good luck to them" said Jen benevolently "That's nice! What are we going to do with it?"

"Not sure" he replied "but we're definitely eating out tonight!"

Jack looked Simon over. They had done a good repair, and he placed the pig back in his corner.

Jen poked her head round the corner, "Perhaps we should invite Ted & Rosemary out for a meal at the Tortilla Shed tonight?"

"Really?" replied Jack, unconvinced "They can afford to dine out themselves!"

"That's not the point. It'd be by way of a thank you"

"Marty as well?" Jack asked, hoping for a "no".

"Yes!" said Jen "the whole family"

"Lovely" said Jack.

" . . . and sizzling fajitas for me, please" said Jen to the waiter at the Tortilla Shed, a reasonably priced, good Mexican restaurant tastefully themed with coloured tiles, wooden floors and mariachi music.

"To Ted!" Jack said raising his glass smiling "who seems to be mellowing in his old age"

"Jack!" chastised Jen.

"No, I mean it" continued Jack, looking at his brother, "I'm pleased for your win and thank you"

"Yes, to Ted!" smiled Jen

"To the Piggy Bank" shouted Marty, Teds youngest, wanting to join in the grown-up toasting. "*The Piggy Bank*!" he shouted, chuckling.

"Quiet" snapped Rosemary in barely concealed annoyance, "Remember what we said."

"Piggy Bank, Piggy Bank!" he shouted, enjoying saying what he wasn't allowed to say at the top of his voice.

"Ok, young man, if you can't behave you're outside with me!" said Rosemary dragging him out to the play area as diners looked on in equal measures of annoyance and amusement.

"Piggy Bank?" asked Jack

"Yes" laughed Ted trying to lighten the moment "he's just got a new china piggy bank and it's turned his head! He can't stop talking about it, and you know what they're like! Tell them to stop and they take it up a level!"

Ted sipped his bottle of beer discretely checking people's eyes for levels of concern, but the incident seemed to have passed without suspicion.

Five minutes later, mother and child returned, Marty looking suitably chastised his mouth now occupied with an ice lolly.

Actually the evening progressed reasonably well. The two families chatting amicably enough, Ted even reminding Jack of some old times at home when they were young "Remember that bike you went straight over the handle bars on Jack?" asked a beer-fuelled Ted . "Yes!" smiled Jack, "only because you threw the stick in the spokes". They hadn't laughed like that for some time.

Marty had calmed down now, tiredness getting the better of him.

"I fancy some fresh air" announced Jack "do you fancy playing on the slides outside Marty?" There was nothing unusual in that as Jack enjoyed playing with his nephew, "keeps him off the furniture" he'd think.

"OK" said Rosemary "But behave yourself Marty, and remember what we said". Marty nodded and didn't seem as hyped up as before.

In the restaurant play area, Marty was enjoying himself on the slide.

"Ouch!" he screamed.

"Are you alright?" said Jack.

"The slide pulled my plaster off!" said Marty on the verge of crying, holding his hand.

"You're alright" reassured Jack sitting him on his knee and putting the plaster back on as best he could.

"That pig cut me it did Uncle Jack"

"Ah, yes" said Jack "looks like its healing up nicely though"

"Mum calls it the Piggy Bank!" smiled Marty.

"What? *Your* piggy bank" asked Jack

"No, Simon silly!"

"Oh?"

"'Cos of the money that came out of it . . . like a piggy bank! Ha, ha, ha!" he laughed, the cut to his hand a distant memory.

"Oh, mummy and daddy found some money *inside* Simon did they?" asked Jack, things now making sense.

"Yes and they got a nice new car!"

"Yes, they *did*, didn't they" agreed Jack, remarkably calmly.

His brother hadn't mellowed at all and Rosemary had never been a force for good in their relationship.

"I like Simon!" beamed Marty "I like his eyes. They're so twinkly!"

Inevitably, the incident further soured Jack and Ted's relationship. Ted and Rosemary eventually gave most of the money back and, after some time, the couples started talking again. Marty had actually missed his uncle and aunty. But it would never be the same.

As young Marty had noticed, Simon's eyes were indeed rather special. The Columbian's would have paid a lot more than Jack's original three pounds to get them back. Two rare black opal stones . . . and £800,000 of their money was tied up in them. Just sitting there. Simon would continue to look out over Jack and Jen's living room for a few more years and whenever Marty would visit, he would always comment on their twinkle . . . so much that eventually Jack decided to get them properly evaluated. Eventually, what the Columbians had hoped to enjoy, Jack and Jen actually did. Of course, they had Simon's eye's professionally replaced, with some black onyx stones, far less valuable but they retained some of Simon's original twinkle. Marty couldn't tell the difference.

Understandably, Jack and Jen didn't feel the need to share their good fortune with Ted and Rosemary. A modest lottery win they said . . . and Ted and Rosemary tried so hard to look pleased for them, they almost succeeded.

Gobbi Bonjour

"Welcome Gobbi! Do you mind me calling you Gobbi?" asked Morag Style as she started her radio interview.

"Of course not! It's my name! *You* must get some stick for *Miss Style!*"

"Ahh, indeed I have in the past!" laughed Morag in her Scottish lilt.

Morag continued: "Now, I don't want to dwell on it, but your name *is* unusual. For our listeners who don't know you, and there can't be many, could you explain how it came about?"

"Nothing unusual really" he smiled "My father was Moroccan—that's the Gobbi—and I'm going to let you guess where my mother was from!"

"Ah, let me see" joked Morag "would it be Ireland?"

"Sacre bleu!" laughed Gobbi "So you see I've got my parents to blame! It trips off the tongue though, don't you think?"

"It does indeed, as if you were *born* to host a game show. You do it so *well!*" replied Morag, a big fan and a little bit under his spell.

"You are too kind" he smiled, looking every inch the young game show host, immaculately dressed in a tailored suit and tie. He had just the right tan to highlight his perfect white teeth and he was very comfortable being interviewed, particularly by a woman.

"So this new show of yours, *The Money or a Life,* was it your idea?"

"No, no!" replied Gobbi, "I wish it was! I'd be a rich man! Some bright spark at the network . . . it is *genius* though, don't you think?"

"Oh, I absolutely *love it!*" replied Morag "and it's the perfect match for you!"

Gobbi's ego was being well and truly massaged.

"It's such fun to do Morag, and we've had such good feedback. You just have to look at the ratings!"

"It does seem to have captured people's imaginations" said Morag.

"It's such a great concept isn't it" replied Gobbi, "and everyone can relate to it—*everyone's* got relatives and a family".

"That's definitely the beauty of it" said Morag. "Now, for the few people who *haven't* seen it, we've got a clip from the show"

"Oh great" said Gobbi, genuinely looking forward to hearing the sound of his own voice.

Audience clapping dies down . . .

Gobbi: "OK Kevin, you've done extremely well so far. How are you feeling?"

Kevin: (nervous) "Good, good"

Gobbi: "Well, you've reached the point in the show when I have to ask, will it be . . . (audience joins in) THE MONEY OR A LIFE!"

Kevin: (smiling) "It's a lot of money, Gobbi!"

Gobbi: "It certainly is! £800,000 is a lot of money. So who is your nomination?"

Kevin: "It's my father, Brian" (Brian appears on the big screen).

Gobbi: "Let's hear it for Brian, ladies and gentlemen!" (applause).

Kevin: "He's 87, he says he's had a good life and he reckons he's ready to go".

Brian: (on screen)"That's right. I'm fine with it. I'm thinking what Kevin and the grandkids can do with £800,000! I've had my time".

Gobbi: (smiling to Kevin) "He sounds a lovely man"

Kevin: "He is . . . but of course he's having trouble now. Aren't you Dad? (Kevin shouts at the screen)—HAVING TROUBLE MOVING, EATING, REMEMBERING . . . "

Brian: (in frail voice) "Oh yes, that's true . . . bit of trouble down below too" (audience laugh).

Kevin: (talking to Gobbi) "He says he wants us to have the money".

Gobbi: "Well the decision is yours Kevin . . . will it be (audience joins in) THE MONEY OR A LIFE?!"

"We'll stop it there, Gobbi as I understand that's this week's episode that's going out on Sunday" said Morag.

"Yes, we filmed that last week. Kevin was great!"

"Can you run us through the whole concept then" asked Morag.

"Of course!" he smiled "like a lot of the best ideas, it's really very simple. Our studio guest, gets to nominate an elderly loved one, father, mother, aunt, or such like. Now this is usually someone who has only got a few years to go. We say three years maximum, so they are quite infirm, have health problems, etc. You could say their best years were behind them! Then the guest has to decide whether to choose the money or a life! £800,000 tax free into their account on that day, *providing* the loved one sacrifices their remaining years. As I say, it's a simple concept!"

"Now some people think they die live on TV, in the chair that they are sitting on in the video link, but that's not true is it" said Morag.

"Oh no, of course not!" reassured Gobbi "We did discuss it, but we all agreed it would be in poor taste so it's dealt with in our studios immediately after the show. All very dignified and humane"

"Aye, that is a comfort" agreed Morag, "For me, it's the interplay between the guest and the loved one which is *absolutely fascinating!*"

"I think that *is* the appeal" agreed Gobbi "people *love* to see that". Of course it's rare that people go for it, but when it happens, it is *fantastic television!*"

"Oh it is indeed!" agreed Morag "and we have a clip of the time when that happened last month"

"I thought you would!" laughed Gobbi, "Daryl was incredible wasn't he?! What a moment!"

"Here we go" smiled Morag, "and if you missed this show, you have *got* to listen to this!"

Gobbi: "So who is your nomination Daryl?"

Daryl: "It's my mother, June".

Gobbi: "Let's hear it for June, ladies and gentlemen (audience applauds and cheers as June appears in the big screen). Hello June, and how are you?

June: "Oh, I can't complain".

Gobbi: "You've had a good life then".

June: "Oh yes, very good. But it's getting more difficult now and I'd like my children to have the money".

Gobbi: "Well that's marvellous. £800,000 these days goes a long way.

June: "It certainly does, Gobbi".

Gobbi: "So Daryl, what's it to be? Will it be . . . (audience joins in) THE MONEY OR A LIFE?!"

Daryl looks up at his mother.

Daryl: "I'm choosing . . . " (Daryl pauses and tears run down his face).

"I'm choosing . . . a life" (audience collectively breathes in, in shock).

Gobbi: "Are you absolutely sure, Daryl! It's a lot of money we are talking about here!".

June: (shouting and annoyed) "Daryl, I want you to have the money!"

Daryl: (through tears) "I know you do Mum . . . but I don't want it!" (Daryl sobs)

Audience start to chant. "MONEY, MONEY, MONEY, MONEY!"

Morag fades out the clip, "Absolutely unbelievable scenes!"

"I know!" agreed Gobbi, shaking his head "It doesn't often happen, but when it does, *it's electric!*"

The Bus

2019 timetable
Service: Bus
Arrival: 11.55 13.9.19
Departure: 12 noon 13.9.19

Craig read the bus timetable on the post by the track. It was brief and to the point . . . only one bus that year! But he knew that anyway. There had always only been one bus a year out there. This part of Finland was remote, really remote, which suited him but he wanted to make sure he'd got the right time.

"Twelve on the thirteenth of September" he said to himself deliberately as he wrote it in his small notebook with a stubby pencil. He'd been living in the woods four years now and had become very good at it. If you knew what you were doing, the woods could be a very generous and abundant home, and Craig knew what he was doing. He considered himself a woodsman and did so with some pride, the custodian of skills that most people had forgotten. He was sure he was viewed by some as "sleeping rough" or "homeless" but that didn't concern him. Craig was comfortable and he felt very at home in the forest.

"Time to head back" he thought, looking up at the clear sky as he tucked the notebook and pencil back into his backpack and started to walk south back down the track. Craig had moved around a lot but for the last three months he had settled in a remote glade about six hours walk south of the bus stop. His trip north to the bus stop had been productive as he'd taken the opportunity to collect mushrooms and berries that grew in abundance in this area, but it was time he was getting back. The bus would be arriving in three days and there were things that Craig wanted to get done before then. "Clear out the shelter, use the food".

Over the years, Craig had seen very few people. Two farmers to the West, and two kayakers. He hadn't spoken to any of them and liked to keep his distance, but he remembered the kayakers had made him laugh out loud. Three times they tried to launch into the river, each time capsizing, until Craig was desperate to go down from the hill and help them. But they seemed to get their act together in the end and he knew helping them wasn't very wise.

Craig didn't miss the Army . . . he'd definitely had enough. Even four years later, the nights could be difficult, desert scenes rolling around in his head . . . sand, blood, pain . . . but it *was* getting better. He had killed enough, to the point that now Craig was even reluctant to use his snares. Of course, he knew he had to . . . there were plenty of rabbits and squirrels that were too good to miss.

"What would old Bodger think!" Craig thought smiling as he walked, "Get stuck in!—that's what!" But then killing had always come a little easier to Bodger, he seemed to quite enjoy it. Craig *did* miss his friends . . . "even Bodger, the bloody animal!" he thought. The Army had been a family of sorts for him and he was starting to miss some human contact.

He'd been on his own for a long time and he planned to catch that bus, see where it took him . . . maybe start all over again somewhere. In the Army, there had always been a plan, but Craig hadn't had one for years, his future just blank pages flipping randomly in the wind. But now, he had it in his head to catch that bus.

So over the next two days, he ran down the food supplies in his small shelter. He dismantled the rough timbers that made up the main supports for the walls and the roof and discarded the pine branches that over-laid them to keep out the weather. And at 5.00am on 13th September, he set out back up the track, north to the bus stop.

"It'll be good to talk . . ." he thought as he walked, "just have a conversation about nothing, anything . . ."

With the low morning sun streaming through the trees, he arrived at the stop. Craig crouched behind some bushes just off the road and waited.

Then he heard it . . . the distant clatter of the bus approaching!

"This is it!" he thought, his heart beating faster. It was on time and it pulled up by the post, the folding doors flapping open. Craig could see a few passengers, one standing up and talking to the driver . . .

Call it a sixth sense but Craig couldn't get on that bus. He was desperate to stand up and get on, but somehow he knew it was a mistake. So he stayed behind the bush and, with a heavy heart, he watched as the doors flapped shut and the engine note rose as the bus pulled away. As the dust drifted into the woods, Craig walked into the road to watch the bus disappear.

"Maybe next year . . ." Craig thought as, head down, he set off back down the track. Then he heard the sound of another vehicle . . .

"What?!" he said out loud, knowing there was hardly ever anything on that road. It was the bus reversing back up the road! It squeaked to a stop by the post and the doors flapped open again . . . this time, a backpack hit the ground and a man got off . . . a man he recognised.

"Sherman!" thought Craig frozen to the spot, "What's he doing on a bus?!"

It was a good question. With the might of the military behind him, why *would* he use a bus?! But Craig knew Sherman's methods were unorthodox. He just stood there looking around, taking in his surroundings, like a hunting dog trying to pick up a scent.

"Hasn't seen me" thought Craig, relieved as he thought he might have been spotted on the road. He was well aware of this officer's reputation. Standing there in his sand-coloured army fatigues, Lieutenant Sherman was in no hurry, listening, smelling . . . he knew he'd catch the deserter, he always did. It was just a matter of time.

David

"So, Mr. Morgan" opened the local radio interviewer.

"Robert, please"

"OK, *Robert*. What are you going to *do*?"

"What *can* I do?" replied Robert, "except meet the challenge head on"

"But how do you plan to compete with them?"

"I know what you're going to say" smiled Robert, "Lannda, the fourth largest supermarket, most rapidly expanding, etc, etc. I've heard all the statistics!"

"Forgive me, Mr. Morgan but you seem reasonably cheerful about it!"

"Well it's largely out of my control isn't it!" Robert laughed.

"But you must be concerned after, what, thirty-odd years?"

"Forty-four years last week" said Robert proudly "Twenty with me and twenty-four with my father before me"

"That's fantastic, we *have* had a lot of callers saying your corner shop is a bit of a landmark in Wokeley"

"Well, we've been there a long time and we *do* aim to give a good service. If we haven't got it in stock, we'll get it for you by the next day!"

"What anything?!"

"Pretty much—apart from drugs and weapons maybe!"

"Ha!" the interviewer laughed, caught off-guard by Robert's quip.

"We *have* had a lot of callers talking of Morgan's with great affection"

"That is good to know. We see that from our customers each day. They've become our friends really"

"But returning to my original question Robert, how *are* you going to compete with them opening *right opposite you?!*"

"That *was* a little cruel don't you think?!" laughed Robert "opening *immediately opposite us!*"

"I think that's what has caught people's imagination ... like David and Goliath"

"Yes" smiled Robert "it feels a little like that! Look, *of course*, their stock will be a little cheaper, *of course*, there will be more choice ..."

"*And* the parking is better!" interrupted the interviewer, facetiously.

"Can you believe I was refused a lay-by by the council" laughed Robert "and Lannda have a ground level *and* underground car park! But it's more parking for us too, isn't it!"

"You do seem to be remarkably positive about the whole thing"

"Well, you've got to be haven't you!"

"Some people have wondered whether you received some sort of pay-off from Lannda ... a sweetener?"

"Chance would be a fine thing! That's not their style unfortunately, not very sweet at all. You should have seen the plans they sent me ... our little shop, the road and a *huge* building! Our shop looked like a drain cover next to it!" he laughed.

"Forgive the pun Mr. Morgan but how are you going to stop your business going *down the drain?*"

"Ah, very good" smiled Robert, "We've got to concentrate on the positives"

"Which are?"

"Well, the parking *is* better" Robert joked, "people know us and like us, and people *do* like an underdog here"

"Well, from the sound of our switchboard, they certainly do! So you're not going down without a fight"

"Certainly not!" Robert replied "that's not my style at all. No, we just need to change our strategy slightly, diversify, think of product lines they don't do"

"There can't be many" pointed out the interviewer, holding out little hope.

"True, but we can go for quality and good old fashioned customer service"

"Customer service certainly, but *quality*"? replied the interviewer "from a *convenience store*?! Forgive me, but I thought the whole point was selling cheap items in large volumes?"

Smiling, Robert replied, "as I said, we've been around for a long time and we're going to do our best to meet the challenge".

Robert really wasn't unduly worried. Morgan's had diversified years ago. He'd been a little misleading in his interview about not being able to supply drugs and weapons . . . it had taken a few years but Morgan's really *could* get anything people wanted by the next day. Anything from a tea bag to a bag of something a little stronger, although it was mainly weapons these days. His father had built the business on drugs, but a bad experience, and what was left of his conscience, had turned Robert away from the messier side of the family business, as he saw it. No, he much preferred arms trading . . . more hands-off, vast sums of money traded at a time, at a more comfortable distance. When he'd first seen Lannda's plans, Robert *was* incensed at the injustice, that they had the cheek to open a store immediately opposite! The thought of arranging some sort of incendiary device had even crossed his mind, but that was his heart ruling his head and that never lasted for long.

In reality, Robert knew that Morgan's could import things that Lannda didn't traditionally stock and they had contacts that Lannda wouldn't have.

Despite Goliath, David would be there for a few years to come.

"Safety first, fun later"

"**H**ave you seen this!" gasped Jim, pointing at his paper.

"What's that?" said Austin sipping his pint.

"It's only bloody illegal to put up office decorations at Christmas now! Health & Safety say you can't!"

"That's not quite true, mate" Austin sighed "I wouldn't believe everything you read in the papers, especially that one!"

"Says it right here in black and white!" Jim said handing over the paper.

"Let's have a look" Austin said under his breath. "Yep, as I thought, it's just someone over-reacting, and someone else trying to sell a newspaper!".

"I don't know how you've been involved in it so long, I really don't" said Jim.

"We're not going to do this again are we?" thought Austin.

"There's more to it than you think" Austin replied trying to muster the will to defend his profession again "loads of variety, never a dull moment!"

"Never a dull moment?!"

"I know, I know…" Austin interrupted "Shutting fire doors and showing people how to lift boxes is *sooo* exciting!" It was Jim's favourite wind-up and Austin couldn't help but bite.

Jim laughed "You've got to admit though, it's bloody boring"

"And an IT consultant is just non-stop fun isn't it!" laughed Austin good humouredly, reaching for his pint.

Austin had been a health & safety consultant for years, building up a successful freelance business, and people telling him it was boring pressed all the wrong buttons. The main reason he started the business was to change that image, particularly to inject some life and, where possible, humour into health and safety training. Tricky business as people dying, getting seriously injured or made seriously ill because of their work wasn't a barrel of laughs. But Austin thought it could be presented in a slightly lighter, more digestible way, so people might even think you were a normal person.

This was possibly Austin's trump card, he was pretty normal. *He* wouldn't ban office decorations as it is plainly stupid. He had met some people that *would* though ... safety professionals that owned Volvos, practised fire evacuations in their homes with their kids and risk-assessed the washing-up. But that wasn't Austin. He'd prefer a V8, wouldn't worry about practicing evacuations and try to avoid the washing up. In fact, he had a strong urge to be slightly unsafe in his spare time, some of his previous employers frowning on him riding a motorcycle to work.

But he *did* think it was a reasonable expectation for people to arrive home from work in roughly the same condition as they arrived. That seemed fair to him.

Against all the odds, Austin actually enjoyed his job. He'd fallen into it by accident (he liked that pun) and if anyone had told him in his twenties that a) he'd be in health & safety and b) involved in training, he would have laughed his socks off. Nothing could have been more unlikely, but it had worked out well. Every day different, much more variety than people thought and a real challenge. The most difficult sales job in the world in some respects and he liked the blend of performance and science. All of that and it paid well, gave him plenty of time off and had paid off the mortgage!

But attitudes like Jim's did provoke a reaction ... He understood it as he couldn't remember the last time he had seen a *positive* health and safety related story in the media. Those ones didn't sell papers and sadly everyone had been turned off. It certainly wasn't cool. He even sympathised with some people's views ... "shit happens", "it was just *their time*", "Safety First, Fun later!" ... he was just tired of justifying it, tired of people ranking his profession just below traffic warden and estate agent. Well, traffic warden anyway.

"Next time someone asks me at a party" Austin would think, "I'm telling them I'm a stunt man ... or a firefighter!" He imagined "firefighter" would be a winner "What do I do? Oh, I just save lives on a daily basis ... think of it as a superhero on shifts and you've got it!"

"Must be amazing . . ." he thought.

Today, Austin felt Jim might mention something, he could just feel it in his water. So just for fun, Austin had prepared a short questionnaire. As he took it out of his pocket, it struck him that preparing a short safety questionnaire was a very uncool and dull thing to do, but hey, "Safety first, fun later"

"A *questionnaire*?!" laughed Jim.

"Yeah, a questionnaire" smiled Austin.

"You boring little tit!" he laughed.

"Look, I'm going to the bar to get you a drink and a snack of your choice. You read it and fill it in for me"

"Oh well, if you're buying I'll have the usual, and a packet of cheese and onion crisps please"

Jim unfolded the questionnaire and reluctantly settled down with a pen . . .

For each of the examples, score your opinion on the following scale:

"Shit happens" = Score 1

"That was a little unfair" = Score 2

"Unacceptable" = Score 3

1. *Seventy people burned to death in a fire in a Bangladesh clothing factory, trapped in a huge dead end. Twenty people were found wedged in a doorway after trying to climb over each other. At 8.00pm, when her seventeen year-old daughter Ashita hadn't come home from work, her mother started to worry. Ashita was stuck half-way up the doorway.*

    Score =

2. *Kevin was killed instantly by a train that left the track and mounted the platform, as he sipped a cup of coffee. Kevin had his back to the track and hadn't seen it coming. The worn section of track was known to be faulty for three months but there was an argument about which company was paying for the repair. In two year's time Kevin would have been a grandfather.*

    Score =

3. *Mr and Mrs. O' Doherty's 15 year old daughter, Mandy was on work experience at a warehouse. Mandy was reversed over by an articulated lorry at midday on a sunny day in June. She was killed instantly and it was filmed on CCTV, ending up on You Tube. Mandy was unrecognisable and only identified by dental records. There was just the driver and Mandy in the huge, empty loading area and there was plenty of space, but there was a blind spot that drivers had complained about for about six months, after several close calls. The driver never worked again.*

    Score =

4. *To speed up a demolition job, a manager told Colin's Dad not to clear rubble from the floor of a building after knocking internal brick walls down with his bulldozer. It had been agreed earlier that the weight on the floor had to be kept low by regularly clearing the rubble down a central chute but the job was running late and the company faced a fine built into the contract. The weight of the rubble that built up caused the floor to collapse and Colin's Dad fell through three floors in his bulldozer and was paralysed from the neck down.*

    Score =

5. *At 32, Hilary's boyfriend developed permanent tinnitus from working for years with noisy machinery and vehicles in a mine. Her boyfriend wasn't supplied with any protective equipment and wasn't informed about any danger to his hearing, although the risk was well-known in his industry. Her boyfriend now hears a constant human scream in his head, especially when it's quiet at night.*

    Score =

6. *Bill's son worked as an electrician for two years when he was 18 till he was 20. In that time, Bill's son drilled some walls and boards that contained asbestos. Because of this, his son died on his 47th birthday of mesothelioma, an asbestos-related cancer of the lung linings. Bill outlived his son by 25 years.*

    Score =

7. *Joseph didn't understand why his dad cried so much at home and why him mum and dad argued. One day, on his way home from work, Joseph's dad kept his foot on the accelerator of his car. He sped down*

the hill and drove straight through the site security gates. Joseph's Dad, carried on down the hill and drove through the garden wall of a house, narrowly missing a child playing in the garden. He had snapped after months of bullying, a high work load and working long hours. He needed three months off work to recover and never returned to that company. He was eventually replaced with two people, neither of whom had the experience to do the job as well as Joseph's Dad.

Score =

8.   *To speed up a job, it was known that people sometimes removed a guard on a rubbish compactor and forced the rubbish through some shredder jaws with their legs by standing on top of it. One day, June's husband was doing the same. He'd done it many times and it had been OK. Today, his foot was drawn into the shredder blades drawing both legs in, until his hips jammed the machine. He was conscious all the time until the Fire Service arrived, even managing to phone June while she was at work, but he eventually died from blood loss and shock. A fireman had to cut June's husband's body from the machine by sawing through it at the hips. This affected him quite badly.*

Score=

Now add up your score and see what it says about you . . .

Score 0-9 *"I don't really care. It's just natural selection taking stupid people out of the gene pool"*

Score 10-17 *"Some people are really unlucky, aren't they"*

Score 18-24 *"I love health and safety, I do!"*

"What did you get Jim?" asked Austin returning with the drinks.

"Turns out I love heath and safety, I do! Who'd have thought it!" said Jim "Now hand me those bloody crisps!"

The Cure

Tim opened the front of his damp tent and poked his head out into the September drizzle. The trees on the overgrown grass verge kept most of the rain off but everything still got damp, his tent, the blankets laying on top of it for extra warmth, his bones... It was the first time he'd looked out for three days. There wasn't much reason to as nothing much changed. The two other tents on the verge were still there, still the subway wall that his tent opened onto, still the busy dual carriageway that ran behind the tent beyond the narrow verge. The traffic in the centre of Manchester was always busy but Tim didn't notice it, having tuned it out over the years. Mary still lived in the cardboard wigwam she had built around a tree at the end of the verge. Even though Tim's tent was less than impressive, he considered it far superior to her cardboard "lash-up".

"Even more damp in there, and one gust of wind and it's gone!"

They didn't often talk but Tim liked Mary. There was something about her, something other than the tangle of grey hair and the smell. He had even tried to get a tent for her from social services but he hadn't been successful yet. He'd keep on trying when he could though. Tim didn't often smile but the day when Mary replaced some wet cardboard with an old champagne box did make him laugh. "I'll have some champagne, when you've finished with it Mary!" he shouted, holding his bottle of cheap cider. Mary whooped with laughter.

Life hadn't always been this bleak for Tim. Not that many years ago, he had been a successful biochemist, a respected professor working in the field of antibiotics. He had the recognition of his peers, was published in respected journals, and had sponsorship for his research by government bodies and private companies. He had a marriage ... of sorts. Emma wasn't the love of his life (he'd been too wrapped up in his research to look for, or even notice that) but she certainly fitted into his social circle at the time, a circle that operated in a rarefied atmosphere and included some of the great and the good. He had a house and cars that many would envy ... oh yes, Tim had experienced the trappings of success. But it was amazing how alcohol changed all of that. He had often thought that chemicals, in one form or another, had been the cause of his success *and* his downfall. Some days he would lie there in a haze in his tent, wondering if it was all a dream. He'd started drinking socially, as many do, but Tim's problem was he just couldn't stop at that, until his addiction spiralled out of control and the framework of his life started to fall apart like a stack of cards. Wife, friends, job, professional reputation, it was incredible how quickly they tumbled when faced with his socially unacceptable behaviour, behaviour not becoming of those circles, behaviour that might reflect on *them*. And so began the process of his gradual disassociation, from the spires of the university to the tent on the verge.

Life on the verge wasn't what you would call "sociable". No coffee mornings or dinner parties here, people tended to keep themselves very much to themselves. Tim couldn't remember the last time he'd seen Ray in the tent next door. He didn't get up for long spells, and when he did he could be quite aggressive and had very little to say. He'd once mentioned to Ray he was a biochemist. Ray replied "Of course you were ... and I was a fucking astronaut!" and turned back to his tent.

On a fine day, birds would be singing and, all around them, people would be going about their business, noisy groups of students making their way to the university, planning their weekends, an endless stream of cars passing by on the dual carriageway. "We could be dead in here and no-one would know" Tim would think, looking up at the blue nylon of his tent roof.

There *would* be the occasional visitor, some welcome, but most not. The social workers *were* welcome and normally friendly but they called much less frequently these days. Less welcome were the occasional thieves and abusers but thankfully, Tim could hold his own and the worst that had happened was some booze had been stolen. He had known others in town, in shop doorways and arches, that had been assaulted for no reason, robbed of the little that they had, but most of the time on the verge, they were invisible. People knew they were there but no-one cared, they just walked on, as if Tim, Ray and Mary didn't really exist. Years of being ignored like this had brought on an unsettling sense of isolation in Tim, a growing disconnection from the people who constantly circulated around him, as if he sat in the eye of a storm, everything calm, as time stood still.

Time was the one thing that Tim had in abundance on the verge. All the time in the world it seemed, no structure, no deadlines… The alcohol helped of course with days easily lost in a swirling, soft focus haze. To the passer-by who might shout "get a job!", it probably looked like long spells of inactivity, but it really wasn't for Tim. It was time to *think*, to lose himself in his favourite place, the world of biochemistry. In his head, he had been continuing his research, imagining complex three dimensional molecules slowly spinning through space and working out how they would interact with common harmful bacteria and viruses. He would spend hours doing this, inside his tent, eyes closed in his own world. This ability to visualise complex structures was always a gift since his days at the University. He rarely wrote things down, frustrating students and peers alike.

"You're doing it again Tim! You'll have to use the board to explain it to us mere mortals!" And he found the alcohol helped to free up his thoughts and get him into a more creative state.

The day it came to him was much like any other. But it came like divine intervention, a moment of pure clarity in his little tent on that insignificant verge.

"Oh my God!" Tim didn't believe in one but his Catholic childhood meant it was a default position at times of shock or elation, and this was a bit of both.

"Oh my *God!* I've done it!" He *knew* it would work. He could visualise the floating molecule, interacting with the micro-organism in a way that it could not possibly survive. And the *real* beauty was, there was no reason to think it wouldn't work with most harmful bacteria and viruses! It was the answer to the global problem of antibiotic resistance, the biggest thing since penicillin! The Beatles had written their best songs under the influence of drugs and it seemed that Tim's addiction and isolation had helped create *his* masterpiece!

He scrambled out of his tent.

"Mary!" he called out in excitement. "Mary!"

He pulled back the blanket at the entrance of her shelter. "Mary?!"

Mary was lying motionless, in a foetal position towards the back.

"Oh no" he said under his breath. He rushed over to her but he knew before he moved she was gone.

"Oh, Mary . . ." Overwhelmed with the sadness of the sight of her, Tim wept beside her on his knees for some time, holding her hand.

Eventually, tears stinging his eyes, he walked out into the day.

He looked around at the people and the cars that forever circulated the verge. No-one missed a step and the world carried on as if nothing had happened. Then one person glanced over to him, and just as quickly looked away as Tim caught their eye. He thought of all the people that had looked away in the past, all the people who had turned their backs on him when he needed help.

He looked out and he honestly couldn't see anything worth saving.

"Fuck them" thought Tim.

Barry

Dean knew it was mistake to take the short-cut.

"You know the drill!" smiled the tall, remarkably relaxed mugger, as he blocked Dean's path up the alleyway.

"Money, phone, watch, and fucking be quick about it!" He had the air of an experienced purveyor of menace, perhaps starting to get bored with the whole thing, but it was obvious to Dean he meant business.

"Shit!" Dean realised there wasn't a soul in the alleyway except them.

"Fucking hell, *a badger!*" Dean shouted in surprise pointing towards the ground behind the mugger.

"What the f…" said the mugger. And in that split second of confusion, Dean buried his boot as hard as he could in the mugger's crotch.

He had always thought that shouting something completely random in such a situation might work long enough to create a distraction, and it had worked like a charm!

Dean edged past his moaning assailant and continued up the alleyway.

"Come on Barry" he called.

A badger shuffled out of a doorway and looked up at Dean.

"Come on boy!"

The badger jumped up into Dean's arms. Dean ruffled Barry's fur and they continued on their way.

Excess Baggage

"*Please do not take heavy luggage up the escalator. Please use the lift*" repeatedly announced the overly polite animated projection of a young woman at the foot of the escalator at Kings Cross station.

There was a selection of cafes on the first floor and Mr Oshiro was desperate for a coffee.

"It'll have to be the lift" he announced "Maybe two trips?"

"OK" said Ricki, his eleven year old son.

Mr Oshiro could only fit seven of his wheeled cubic cases in the lift at one time and still leave room for a person.

"Are you alright with the rest?" asked Mr Oshiro.

"Yes" replied Ricki "I'll see you up there"

When all fourteen brightly-coloured cases had been re-united on the first floor, they found an empty coffee table and wheeled them around it like a pile of giant Lego bricks.

"Excellent!" said Mr Oshiro "Let's relax for a moment".

"Why did we need *fourteen* cases Father? *Five* would have been enough" asked Ricki, sounding older than his years.

"Maybe so, maybe so, but like I said, I wanted to be sure we had enough".

"Yes but *fourteen!* I'm glad we don't have to move them any further!"

"No, they'll be fine here now" said Mr Oshiro, "Just right".

It had taken a long time but they had made it and now, late in the afternoon, they were at their journey's end.

"You stay with the bags and I'll get us a drink. What would you like?" asked Ricki's father.

"Black tea please"

"Anything to eat?"

"An apple, please"

"Might need more, there's a bit of a wait now . . ."

"And why are we so early?!" asked Ricki

"Ah well, we did make the connections a bit more quickly than I thought" replied his father already heading for the café.

Their collection of luggage inevitably started to attract some attention from the commuters.

"Travelling light, I see!" nodded a passing lady.

The boy forced a smile.

"Going away for long?!" joked the waiter clearing tables.

Some of the cases were large, some smaller, all bright single colours, some blue, some red, some yellow and some white.

Mr Oshiro returned with their drinks and snacks.

"*Five* cases, wouldn't have attracted so much attention!" said an annoyed Ricki under his breath.

"Certainly so, certainly so, but the more attention, perhaps the less suspicion?" said his father, convinced by his wisdom.

His son wasn't quite so convinced.

"Can you smell them?" asked his son.

"Only a little, people will think the cases are a bit musty that's all" Mr Oshiro smiled, messily eating a pastry.

"They're going to get louder too!" Ricki pointed out.

He didn't like leaving as many things to chance as his father.

"And you couldn't have *picked* any brighter cases?!"

"Calm down!" said his father exhaling flakes of pastry, "people go for bright cases these days, easier to tell it's theirs"

His son shook his head.

As the evening progressed, there were more comments . . .

"You could set up a luggage shop with that lot!"

They even overheard an older couple walking away saying "What is it about the Japanese? Always loads of cases and cameras!"

"Nice!" commented his son, sarcastically.

"Whose idea was this anyway" Ricki asked his father, the comments wearing thin.

"None of your business!" replied Mr Oshiro, his son's cheek starting to annoy him.

"Not yours then?"

"Not completely, no. But you have to admit it is rather elegant!"

"Mmm" replied the non-committal boy. Like many eleven year olds, Ricki wanted to follow in his father's footsteps but he really didn't like his lack of thoroughness. He preferred to plan more carefully, a trait that would eventually take him a long way in the organisation.

The evening rush hour subsided, the station falling progressively quieter until, in the early hours of the following morning, there was hardly anyone around.

"Good evening sir" said the patrolling Transport Police Officer.

"A good evening to you too Officer" replied Mr Oshiro.

"Missed your train?"

"No, no, just waiting for something" replied Mr Oshiro, feeling the top of one of the cases.

"Well the station is closing soon sir and I'm afraid I'm going to have to move you on".

"I'm afraid that's not possible Officer" said Mr Oshiro.

"I've noticed that you *have* been here a while sir, so I'm afraid I'll have to insist. Couldn't you have sent this lot on in advance?"

"Oh no. We need to keep a close eye on our luggage"

"Could I ask what is *in* them sir?"

"Yes, you can ask"

"What is *in* them sir?" asked the Officer with a grimace.

"I'd rather not say" said Mr Oshiro coyly.

"OK, if that's the way it's going to be I'm going to have to carry out a search"

"Which of course is your right, I would expect nothing else, but could I suggest you open a small bag rather than the larger? smiled Mr Oshiro.

"No sir, you may *not* suggest!"

The impatient officer unzipped the top of a large red case. Immediately, thousands of black flies burst out of the case straight into the officer's face.

"They're ready!" shouted Mr Oshiro as he quickly overcame the officer with a deftly depressed pressure point on his neck.

The case had positively erupted with flies, leaving a shallow layer of seething maggots in the bottom.

Mr.Oshiro and his son quickly unzipped the tops of the other cases, flies bursting out of each one.

The cases of maggots had been lightly coated with a particularly unpleasant bacteria which had multiplied in the warmth of the cases, as the maggots developed into flies. Mr Oshiro and his son wouldn't be affected, nor would any of Mr Oshiro's organisation. But many others would.

Anthrax on letters and door handles was all very well. But *flies*, they're a little more difficult to contain and *so* good at spreading disease. Little experts you might say.

Mr Oshiro looked up and smiled as a huge black cloud of flies billowed up, a buzzing, seething mass in the almost empty station. Their work was done.

"Can we go home now? said a bored Ricki, "I'm hungry".

"Come on then" smiled Mr Oshiro, ruffling his son's hair.

Ricki hated that.

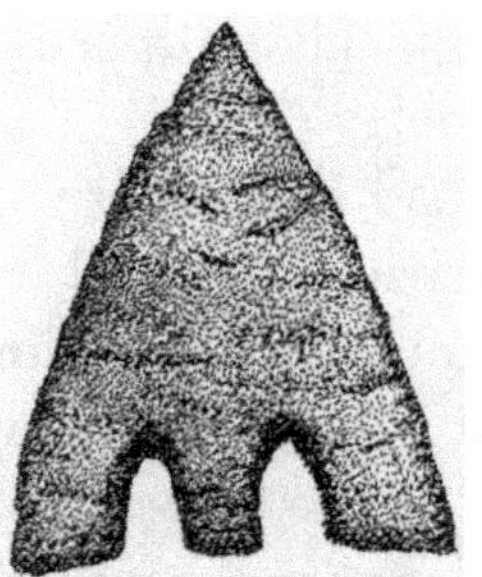

Milestones

1780: "There's a light at the end of the tunnel!" said a relieved Claude to John his workmate as they dropped the penultimate milestone into place. One more to lay and their day's work was done.

"I'll wager we've earned our drinks today!" replied John.

"23 miles to London" said Claude reading the black script on the bright white painted stone, they had placed on the edge of the Great North Road. "Have you ever visited the fair city?"

"No! You can keep it, all the dirt and mess!" replied John "I'm happy with my good lady out here, where the air and the beer is fresh!"

As they loaded their tools into the cart, a robin settled on the stone.

The milestone served travellers well, through beautiful summer days so hot you could hardly touch the stone, and winters so hard the frost would stick your hand to it. Derek wasn't even a twinkle in his parents' eyes yet. Derek's *parents* weren't even a twinkle in *their* parents' eyes . . . but the stone was there. For 120 years it sat there, only occasionally being re-set if its weight had settled it into the ground or the dust from a thousand horses had built up around it.

1904: The first car passed the milestone, a milestone in itself.

1930: Drivers rely on the milestone less and less, eventually hardly giving it a glance. It was becoming a symbol of the past . . . more often a resting place for walkers, a perch for birds, and an occasional obstacle for the inebriated walking down from the Wagon and Horses.

1940: "Doodle bug!" Derek's future father shouted as he ran up the hill from school. The motor of the V2 rocket stopped just above the milestone and dropped ... Derek's future father knew what that silence meant and hit the ground as the deafening explosion destroyed the row of old cottages where he lived. His ears rang for three days. The milestone was chipped by a piece of flying shrapnel but Mrs Jeffers, a neighbour in the end cottage was killed outright, the only person to be hurt by the bomb. Neighbours laid yellow and blue flowers around the milestone, Mrs Jeffer's favourites. The ring of flowers was kept fresh for some months afterwards.

1952: "It's good to be back" smiled Derek's future father. Eventually a new row of houses had replaced the old cottages and the family happily moved out of temporary accommodation and into number seven.

1953: "Where shall we meet then?" asked Derek's future father, excited that Derek's future mother had said yes, she *would* come out with him.

"How about the milestone?" she said "I'll be there at half five, straight after work"

"This is it!" thought Derek's future father at the stone as he watched Derek's future mother walk up the hill, resplendent in a cream dress with red roses.

1963: "It's a boy!" said the midwife to Derek's mother. In February, with the milestone encrusted in frost, Derek was born. It was a very hard winter and for two months after, the milestone was buried in snow.

1971: "Get back from the road!" shouted Derek's mother as he played Hopscotch over the stone just down from their house, "How many times do I have to tell you!"

That same year Derek was excited to see the stone being repainted.

"It looks like new!" he ran to tell his mother.

But gradually Derek took less notice of the milestone, his priorities overtaken by football, toys, friends and then girls. There were pictures of footballers and cars on his wall, but no milestones. In fact, these days it was rare for *anyone* to notice the stone ... very few people needed reminding that it was 23 miles to London.

1985: "I do!" Derek told Penny enthusiastically at the altar. They soon moved further up the A10, further from London where the house prices were much cheaper. They were very happy in their new lives. Derek didn't give the milestone a thought for years. But there it still sat.

2002: "50 years since I met you at that milestone, do you remember?" smiled Derek's father to his mother.

"Yes I *do* remember!" she beamed. Recalling things from years ago was fine, it was the last fifteen minutes that she struggled with. She would only be in the house for three more months.

2003: The hearse carrying Derek's mother passed the milestone. Derek noticed it out of the window for the first time for years, smiling through tears, as he remembered his Mum chastising him for playing on it.

2005: Derek came to a milestone of sorts. "Life's too short" he started to say, although Penny would tell her friends that it was a mid-life crisis.

They started to travel more, something he had always meant to do, and he consciously worked less hours, avoiding the overtime.

Even got himself a motorbike—nothing flash, an old Honda he had always liked from his teenage years but hadn't had the money to buy.

He loved it and often passed the milestone on the Great North Rd, the road little used now since the village was by-passed years ago by the new road.

2007: He was really unlucky to hit the stone that day. It was cold but it wasn't wet and he'd ridden that road hundreds of times. To slide *so far* along the road, and for his head to hit *that* stone … it was more likely he'd be struck by lightning.

As he lay there for a moment, Derek could see something … "There's a light at the end of the tunnel …" he said into his helmet. Derek's last breath misted up his visor on that crisp December morning.

As the visor cleared, a robin settled on the milestone, just as they always had.

The Joker

"My wife was at a party, telling people how she'd invented the echo . . ." said Tyler.

Mr. Renfield smiled, hooked by the joke immediately.

". . . and I said, just listen to yourself!"

Mr Renfield exploded into laughter, the punchline delivered like its namesake, a punch to the gut causing him to involuntarily exhale. He reeled back, gasping in air and roared with spontaneous laughter, doubling him in spasms and contorting his face into a wide-eyed clown grin.

"That's!..That's the . . ." Mr Renfield just couldn't get his words out.

That's . . . *the funniest thing I have ever heard!*" He squeaked, losing all his breath again, his face bright red, veins protruding on his forehead.

"I thought you'd like it!" smiled Tyler.

"*Like it?!*" wheezed Mr Renfield, unable to stop laughing, "*Like it?!. . . I love it!*"

He really couldn't stop, " . . . *just listen to yourself!*" he roared.

"I really must be going now" chuckled Tyler "I'll let myself out and I'll be in touch soon"

"Oh thank you . . ." said Mr Renfield "*Thank you!*" he blurted, unable to contain himself "*Goodbye!*"

"Goodbye Mr Renfield". As Tyler shut the door he could still hear Mr Renfield giggling halfway down the stairs.

A full ten minutes later, the joke almost out of his system, Mr Renfield made himself a cup of tea to wet his sore throat. He felt good, "It *is* the best medicine!" he smiled to himself.

Later that night, Mr Renfield passed away quietly in his sleep. The autopsy would show a small brain aneurism, a very slow bleed caused by the paroxysms of laughter from earlier. It was a kind exit, just going to bed feeling good . . . and not waking up.

Back in his Chelsea flat, overlooking the river, Tyler's next job beeped onto his computer screen. "Here we go again" he smiled, settling in front of the screen. A middle-aged banker . . . he had seen many similar before, this one lined and slightly bloated. Tyler's services were unique, clean and in big demand.

"*Loading*" flashed on his screen as the image of his next target was uploaded into Tyler's programme, a unique digital tool that read microscopic features of a person's face and then matched a joke to their specific character, a killing joke that would induce a fatal reaction. It had taken Tyler years to perfect but, for the last three years, it had worked flawlessly. In ten minutes, the programme would produce a joke that would reliably induce the haemorrhage some hours later.

Tyler felt quite at ease with his version of "assassin". No struggles, no blood, no threat, just orchestrating a meeting and guiding the conversation so that his lines could be delivered. It would normally start in the guise of a business meeting, slowly gaining his victim's confidence . . . until the punchline was delivered with impeccable timing. He would leave to the sound of his victim laughing out loud . . .

"How many assassins can say that!" thought Tyler, "so much kinder than a gun, a knife or a piano wire", he reflected as the banker's joke fell into the tray of the printer.

Room 102

"Ah, it's Donald isn't it?" said the immaculately suited junior minister.

"Yes it is" nodded Donald as he took in the dark oak-panelled grandeur of Room 102, an office in the basement of the Houses of Parliament.

"You are very welcome young sir" said the minister, shaking his hand, "please come in and take a seat"

Donald smiled as he breathed in the age of the room. He settled himself into the deep-buttoned Chesterfield chair opposite the desk and three huge oil portraits looked down on him.

"Hula hoop?" offered the minister, gesturing towards the silver tray on his desk displaying all three flavours, ready salted, cheese and onion and barbeque.

"No, I'm fine thanks"

"Sorry, bit of a weakness I'm afraid" smiled the minister reaching for the barbecue flavoured packet and pulling it open.

"Now, did you enjoy your tour?" he smiled.

"Very much so" enthused Donald "I've been very well looked after . . . and what a building!"

"Yes, it *is* a bit of a show-stopper isn't it—we Brits do the pomp and circumstance so well don't you think? Costs the taxpayer a bloody fortune though! Do you know how much was spent on the east wing this year?"

"Er no?"

"No, you don't want to either!" said the Minister spluttering on his snack, "Robbery it was! Will you join me in a coffee or tea?"

"Oh, a coffee would be nice, thank you"

"Splendid!" said the minister, pouring from the coffee pot on his desk, prepared earlier by his secretary.

"Now, I hear congratulations are in order!"

"Well, it's early days but yes, they could well be" smiled Donald.

"I think you're being modest with me" smiled the minister, passing the coffee. "I would certainly like to extend the hearty congratulations of Her Majesty's Government on your work"

"Thank you very much" blushed Donald.

"Something about a breakthrough with vitamin C, I hear? You don't mind do you?" he asked as he picked a cigar from a wooden box.

"Not at all". The smell of a cigar had always reminded Donald of his grandfather.

"One for yourself, Donald?"

"No, thank you"

"So, talk me through it…what stage are you at?" he asked lighting the cigar.

"Well, we've not gone public yet…"

"Very wise, very wise"

"…but we really think we have something"

"It certainly sounds like it" nodded the minister, puffing on his cigar "Tell me more, it's always good to hear it from the horse's mouth, so to speak!"

"It's remarkably simple really—like most good ideas, I suppose" Donald continued.

"Not *all* though!" the minister interrupted with a raised finger "What about manned space flight—good idea, remarkably complicated!"

"Quite" agreed a bemused Donald.

"The tax system!" said the minister "Bloody good idea…bloody complicated!"

"I'm sorry Donald, please continue" he waved, drawing on his cigar.

"My team and I have discovered that very high doses of vitamin C, destroy cancer cells".

"Not the first time that has been tried is it?" stated the minister.

"No, once before in Norway but we're using much higher doses—many, many times in excess of the recommended daily intake".

"Mmm . . . so you flood the body with vitamin C then, bathing the tissues, veritably filling a chap from the boots up with the stuff!" laughed the minister.

"Well yes, exactly that!" laughed Donald, "but it's the *length* of treatment too. We've found that, to be fully effective, it has to continue for three months"

"And, just to be clear, Donald, it's *just* vitamin C, nothing else?"

"No that's the beauty of it!" It works! It really works!" beamed Donald.

"Yes, so I've heard" said the minister, his gaze fixed beyond the office walls, exhaling smoke . . .

"This is Nobel Prize material you know"

"Well, I don't know about that" said Donald with slightly false modesty.

"No, I really think you have a chance—quite visionary" assured the minister.

"How many in your research team?"

"Only three"

"Very wise, very wise. Keep it close. Easier to control"

"Yes, that was the idea, a very small focussed team"

"Perhaps we should have invited the whole team today? I'll get Penny to arrange a later visit"

"That's very kind, I'm sure they'd enjoy it" encouraged Donald.

"Yes, maybe so . . . " the civil servant said distantly. "Do you play darts Donald?" he said, snapping back into the room.

"Er, no" replied Donald, more of a rugby man.

"Oh, I *love* darts! Come here, I'll show you!"

A dartboard hung on the oak panelling, obviously well-used. The back panel was missing and all around the board the oak was lightly splintered from hundreds of unsuccessful throws.

The minister took his place at the line on the deep carpet and leaned forward.

"Now, I might be missing something here, so bear with me" he said, cigar in the corner of his mouth.

"But vitamin C is fairly cheap, isn't it". He took aim.

"Yes" confirmed Donald.

"And plentiful?" His dart thudded into double top.

"Oh, yes, you can grow it, of course!" The minister's second dart hit the centre of triple twenty.

"Very few side-effects?" he said turning to Donald.

"Worst is an upset stomach!" smiled Donald.

His third dart thumped into the bull's eye.

"You see where I'm going with this Donald?"

"Er . . . no, not really sir"

"*Sir!*" "Oh no! You'd have thought so by now, wouldn't you! Maybe next year!" laughed the minister removing his darts from the board.

"No, what I'm driving at is . . . and if you were American you could say this was the $64,000 question . . . "Where's the money in it?"

"Money?"

"Yes Donald! The *money* . . . where is it? I'm having trouble seeing any"

The minister passed the darts to Donald.

"Well . . . " thought Donald, taken aback, "there are obvious savings. It *is* very cheap, as you say. Much less cost to the NHS compared to existing treatments, no unpleasant side-effects. Ultimately less people to treat through the system . . . I am sure we are looking at a cure!"

Donald's first dart missed the board and hit the oak panel, the conversation affecting his aim.

"Donald, you've just said it yourself" replied the minister "*less cost!* Where is the money in that? *Cancer treatments—a lot of money* involved. *Charities—*a lot of money involved. *Running the NHS—a lot of money* involved"

"I think we could save a huge amount" reassured Donald, the defence of his work now distracting him from the game.

"I agree! Quite so! But, I don't think you're seeing the bigger picture here. There are, shall we call them, *beneficiaries* of the system. *Important* beneficiaries" The minister walked back to his desk to take a sip of coffee.

"You're right of course—it is, as they say, a no brainer! So much to gain, for so little. But, with the greatest respect Donald, you are removing a demand . . . and removing a *fear!* All very laudible, but with that, you are *removing* money from the system! And these people *don't like* to lose money, Donald. Trust me, they get twitchy about losing *any* . . . I was talking to one the other day and he was mortified about a 2% drop in some shares!"

Donald was confused. "But you can't just see it in financial terms!"

"Of course not, Donald, and they *do* see a broader picture . . .
they're also thinking *there's too many people in the world*—a population explosion, I think they call it . . . *so why save everyone?*

The minister let the question hang in the air with his cigar smoke.

Donald smiled as the penny dropped "Ahh, I get it!" he laughed "Very funny! Where's the hidden camera then, in the paintings?!"

The minister smiled and shook his head. He wheeled around and threw a dart at full force into Donald's chest. The nerve toxin took effect almost instantly, dropping Donald to the floor, the darts rolling out of his hand onto the carpet.

Picking up the darts, the minister continued.

"I expect you've been wondering who they are Donald?" said the minister pointing towards the oil portraits above his desk.

"Well that chap invented the car that ran on water. Genius! And the chap next to him . . . he actually manufactured an ever-lasting battery!"

Donald's face was flushed . . . he couldn't speak and was finding it difficult to breath.

"She was a stubborn one!" pointed the minister to the lady on the right,
" . . . no such thing as global warming indeed!"

Donald pulled at his shirt collar.

"Visionaries all!" proclaimed the minister "And *your* picture will hang alongside them, Donald, rest assured"

"And it's not that your research won't be *used*. I *guarantee* that it will be—it's just that less people will be benefitting than you thought"

As Donald lost consciousness, the minister tipped the last of the Hula Hoops into his hand and knelt down beside him.

"On behalf of Her Majesty's Government, *thank you* Donald . . . for your valued contribution."

Tony

"How's Dad?" asked Tony from the back of the car.

"He's fine" replied his mother Florence from the passenger seat, "he sends his love but he's very busy."

Florence and her older son Terry always took Tony for a drive round the rolling grounds of the Institution when they visited. Forty-five now, it had been his home for thirty-three years and he was happy there. Tony's entrance into the world had been difficult. The blood flow to his brain had only been restricted for a few minutes, but it was enough to cause some learning difficulties and to severely affect his sight. "Probably wouldn't happen now", the doctors had said to Florence, which was cold comfort.

Tony was sent to the Institution aged twelve. It was a difficult time for Florence...just after the war, trying to make ends meet, husband away with his driving job, knowing about his affair... in the end she just couldn't cope. Terry missed having his brother around when he left, but he wasn't that far away and he and his mother visited once a month...when they could.

"When is Dad coming to see me?" asked Tony.

Florence looked across to Terry. "He will soon, but he's very busy with work. He sends his love though"

"Oh", Tony smiled and looked out of the car window, through the streaking droplets of rain. Tony's Dad had died five years ago, but no-one had the heart to tell him, for fear it would break his heart.

Terry continued the slow drive around the winding parkland roads.

"Do you remember that time you put the garden fork through your wellies, Tone?"

"Yes!" laughed Tony, a huge grin over his full face.

"The look on your face! You just stood there, thinking you'd put it straight through your foot! Do you remember it went right between your toes?!"

"Yes!" he giggled, his breath starting to steam up the windows.

Terry always reminded Tony of that story and they'd all smile as they remembered some good times at 82, their old house … the swing, the orchard …

"And me shooting the apple off Pat's head … do you remember that Tone?!"

"Yes!" he giggled.

"She must have been ruddy mad to agree to it!" said Florence sternly, but she knew Terry was a good shot.

The cloth squeaked across the windscreen as Terry cleared the condensation from inside.

"It's that mouse in the car again Tone!"

"No!" smiled Tony, looking down. He could see very little these days.

"It *is*, listen …" Terry squeaked the cloth, "There it is! Make sure it doesn't go up your jumper!"

Tony giggled until he turned red.

The rain eased and Terry pulled up outside the entrance of the house.

"Have you got my ciggies and sweets?" asked Tony.

"Yes, these should keep you going" said Terry, passing them to him. "Are you keeping them somewhere safe so you don't lose them?"

"Yes" smiled Tony, cuddling them to his chest.

"Look after yourself then" said Florence, giving him a hug. There may have been a tear in her eye but it never showed.

"We'll see you soon, dut".

The care assistant took Tony's arm to lead him inside.

"Come on Tony, there's a nice cup of tea for you inside".

"Thank you" gestured Terry as he led his mother back to the car.

Tony was pleased to hear his Dad was well.

His condition helped as he didn't dwell on things for too long but, in quieter moments, he *did* sometimes wonder why his Dad was always too busy to see him …

J

"I've bought you a CD to listen to" said Janet as she sat next to Julian in his room at the care home. "Can you guess what songs are on there?

"All the songs in the world!" Julian laughed. He was prone to act quite manically and would often impulsively exaggerate.

"What *every one*?!" humoured Janet, knowing how he could be.

"Yes that's right, *all* the songs in the world! Ha, ha, ha!"

"I don't think we'd get *all* of them on the disc, Julian"

"*I* can!"

"Really?!" laughed Janet "I didn't know you were a computer expert in your spare time! You'll have to come round and have a look at mine, it's been playing up!"

Janet had other patients to look after but she did enjoy spending time with Julian. There was something about his playful innocence she really liked.

And Julian was very happy at the home. He was well-liked by staff and patients and it was his whole world, not appearing to have any other visitors or family. He did enjoy the bus trips that the home organised and he spent a lot of time on his laptop.

"What have you learned this week on that computer of yours then Julian?" asked Janet.

"Oh, lots" he smiled "I was looking at torque converters"

"Talk converters? I could do with one of those for Ronald down the corridor! Haven't got a clue what he's on about!"

"No!" shrieked Julian "*Torque* converters—from automatic gearboxes, silly!"

Janet was surprised he was interested in something so technical.

"Julian, sometimes I wonder why you need this place at all! I could still use that *talk* converter though!" she laughed.

"I think I've made a bit of a mess, can you help me please?" said Julian concerned.

"Of course, let's get you sorted" reassured Janet, switching into care mode.

Later that evening, Julian was tapping away on his laptop as usual, headphones in his ears. He opened a link to the base on his home planet, Faro in the Andromeda galaxy, and downloaded the contents of Janet's disc into the Music file. All of the songs in the world *were* on there . . . he really could do anything with computers, especially this one . . . it was as complex to him as using a paper clip. J smiled as he opened the Engineering file and entered some basic information about torque converters. He was surprised how rudimentary our modes of transport were. "At this rate it'll be four hundred years before they even consider atomic vibration!" he thought.

The care home was a perfect base for J. No-one asked questions and it seemed that occasional manic behaviour and loss of bowel control was all that was needed to continue his work undisturbed.

"Thank you J" came back the message from Faro, "Another lunar month and we should have all the information we need".

"I think I can do it in three of their weeks!" boasted J, the exuberance of youth, clouding the enormity of his task.

"Possibly—remember it's easy to gather the information that *they* know but we'll need more time for *our* research" came back the message, "so take your time there, *take your time*".

J's trip from Andromeda was fairly routine but still involved a manipulation of time that was never taken lightly.

There was a knock on the door.

Julian shut his laptop and popped his head round the door.

"There's some hot chocolate in the lounge, if you'd like some Julian" said Janet.

"Thank you, I think I will"

J was looking forward to going home but there were two things he would miss the most . . . hot chocolate, and Janet.

Open Wide

Wide-eyed, the little boy held out his small bag of white chocolate buttons and offered one to Keith as they waited in the
dentist's reception.

"Oh, no thank you" he smiled, touched by his generosity. His mother
laughed and lifted him further back into the soft chair.

Keith laughed along with her, "Any other time, I would, but *now!..*"

Wearing a slightly too tight white coat, Miss Welsh entered the waiting
room and handed some notes to the receptionist through the sliding
window.

"Mr Hedges" she beckoned, holding the door open.

Keith smiled politely, stood up and made his way to the treatment room.

In the past, there was always something that needed doing to his teeth,
at least a scale and polish, perhaps a filling coaxed out by a toffee, but
today he was confident it was going to be a clean bill of health.

"Take a seat" Miss Welsh smiled. She had been Keith's dentist for years
but all he knew of her was she was about fifty, had a cat, had a good sense
of humour and her white coat was often slightly too tight . . . and not
always in a good way.

"How are you today, Mr Hedges?"

"Good thank you" A visit to the dentist held no real dread for Keith.

"I heard on the radio it's supposed to be the warmest November since
records began" said Miss Welsh, adjusting the chair backwards.

"It *has* been amazingly mild lately hasn't it?" Keith was quite pleased the small-talk was being covered before he had to reply with Miss Welsh's hands in his mouth.

"If you could just pop these glasses on please . . . and open wide for me". Keith did as he was told.

As Miss Welsh tapped her way through Keith's collection of teeth, she started communicating with her assistant in their unique language "Number 10 present, number 9 missing, number 8 lingual amalgalm, 5, 4, 3, 2, 1, 2, 3, 5 missing, 6, buckle resin . . ."

This process always made Keith smile but now wasn't the time.

"Would you like to rinse out?" offered the not-unattractive assistant.

"No, that's fine thanks". Keith was more of a man than that.

"You're busy today" Keith commented to fill a silence.

"Yes" replied an annoyed Miss Welsh, "It's like a kindergarten out there today isn't it with all the toys on the floor!"

It's no problem" replied Keith "although one boy *did* offer me some chocolate buttons just before I came in!"

"Chocolate buttons!" the words seem to catch in Miss Welsh's throat. "*Chocolate buttons*, in *my practice!*"

"I won't be a moment" she said curtly, to her assistant, putting her instruments down.

Miss Welsh opened the door to reception and surveyed the floor strewn with toys. There was only one child in the waiting room and she fixed him in her gaze and pointed.

"Was it you?!" she spitted.

The boy looked like a rabbit caught in headlights.

"What do you mean?" asked his mother, scooping him up.

"I would be grateful if your child didn't offer my patients *chocolates* before their appointment!"

"Now hold on a second, he was only being generous!"

"And where did he get the sweets *from* I wonder?!" she said shaking her head in disapproval.

"I really object to your tone!" shouted the mother in shock.

"I really object to you! *Sweets* in a dental surgery!!" Miss Welsh tutted.

"Come on, Anthony, we don't have to listen to this!" Anthony was still in the headlights.

"I hope you're satisfied! That's two customers you've lost AND I'll be telling all my friends!"

"Lost! What have I lost?! An ignorant woman and a child who feeds my patients sweets!" she laughed "And you can clear this mess up before you leave!" she shouted before slamming the door.

Covering her son's ears, the mother screamed *You can stick the toys up your uptight arse!"*

A red-faced Miss Welsh re-entered the treatment room. This time Keith looked like the rabbit. He and the assistant had heard everything.

"Now, where were we" she smiled to her grinning assistant.

"I wish I hadn't mentioned it!" blurted Keith.

"No, you did the right thing Mr Hedges"

"I think you may have over-reacted slightly!"

"We care about dental health in this practice" said Miss Welsh as she settled into her chair and re-organised her tools.

"Of course, but I reckon you've lost a customer there" Keith laughed.

"Yes, one that I could do without!" the dentist replied annoyed.

"But . . . " Miss Welsh interrupted, holding the drill.

"Mr Hedges, you might be wise to reconsider prolonging an argument with your dentist!"

"That sounds like a threat!" joked Keith.

"Does it?" Miss Welsh smiled distantly, her eyes staring at the wall. Looking over to her assistant, who smiled in acknowledgement, Miss Welsh buzzed through to reception "Could you hold my patients for the next twenty minutes please"

Keith was confused. "It's not going to take that long is it?!"

Before he could move, the assistant operated a button under the bench that pulled three thick leather straps across his shins, hips and shoulders. They automatically ratcheted tight until he was firmly secured in the reclined chair.

"What the fuck is this!" shouted Keith.

Miss Welsh quickly secured another thick strap manually across his forehead and held a hand over his mouth.

"Nurse, the screens please!" smiled Miss Welsh.

"Ohh good! Excited, her assistant pressed the red button on her desk and four thick screens slowly descended from the ceiling to the floor, more than sufficient sound-proofing for any waiting patients.

Miss Welsh lifted her hand from his mouth.

"What the fuck is going..."

The assistant interrupted Keith by pulling open the poppers on her white coat to reveal a laced basque, accompanied by stockings and suspenders surrounding a figure that Keith had previously not noticed. He was finding it difficult not to notice now. As Miss Welsh calmly organised her tools, her assistant strutted in front of Keith, leaned over and kissed him fully on the lips.

"Before it all starts to get too messy" she smiled, her lipstick smudged across her mouth, now a little less sexy and more deranged clown.

"We'll just pop this in to keep your mouth open" said Miss Welsh expertly inserting the device.

"Now, let's have a look at these teeth then shall we Mr Hedges"

Keith shouted and struggled but the straps held tightly.

"That's a nasty hole in your tooth"

"There'sh no hucking hole!" Keith replied, muffled.

"I'm sorry, I didn't quite catch that"

"I think he said there's no fucking hole" said her assistant frowning at his language.

"Yes there is!" smiled Miss Welsh, "Just here!"

Miss Welsh drilled straight through one of Keith's front teeth, on the gum-line, straight through the nerve, allowing the drill to linger and rock in the hole. It was a technique she had perfected over time to cause maximum pain.

Keith was instantly rigid with pain, like a cold steel spike had been driven up into his brain, overwhelming every other function, speech, breathing...

"Try not to move Mr Hedges, you'll only make things worse"

As his eyes twitched, Miss Welsh withdrew the drill from the hole, the stretched belts creaking as some of their tension eased. Keith gulped in some air, drenched in sweat.

"Now we really ought to do something about that sore gum"

"It'll only get worse if we leave it" nodded her assistant.

"Keep his head still, please nurse"

"Love to". She strutted over and held both sides of his head with her long-nailed hands "Do try to keep still" she said, kissing him on the forehead.

Miss Welsh ran the drill over his top gum, twisting the gum tissue up like spaghetti on a fork.

Keith wept in pain, the blood now making it difficult to breathe.

"Suction, please nurse!"

The assistant hooked the suction tube over Keith's cheek and gurgled away the froth of blood and sputum.

"That's better, now we can see what we're doing"

Reception buzzed through: "Mr Williams has arrived for his 2.30 appointment"

"That's fine, thank you Marcie" replied Miss Welsh.

"Sadly we haven't got all day and all good things must come to an end" said Miss Welsh as she started to clean her instruments, "It was fun though wasn't it?!"

"Ooh yes!" agreed the assistant, buttoning up her white coat, "I love it! Helps the day fly by!"

Keith groaned almost unconscious with pain.

"Give him a shot to settle him down a little" said Miss Welsh as she moved the overhead lamp very close to Keith's face.

The injection took effect almost immediately and as the pain subsided, he could feel the gentle heat of the lamp on his face, halfway between sleep and reality. Miss Welsh pulled her chair up close to Keith's head and he could feel her warm breath on his ear . . .

"You will remember nothing of this, you will not even remember you have been to the dentist. You will feel very little pain as a result of what has happened today. In a moment, I am going to count backwards and, with every count you will feel more relaxed and fall into a contented sleep . . . *ten, nine, eight* . . . you are feeling very good . . . *seven, six, five, four* . . . your muscles are relaxed and you feel a warm comforting glow . . . *three, two* and *one*".

Keith lay completely relaxed, breathing deeply, a normal pallor returning to his face as Miss Welsh removed the straps and started to make him look a little more presentable.

"He'll be out for while" said Miss Welsh "We'll prop him in the cupboard and deal with him later"

Keith woke up sitting on a bench in the park.

"Must have dozed off" he smiled. It was six o'clock on a still summer's evening and he felt good. His mouth felt a little odd, but there was no pain and he remembered nothing. Feeling refreshed, he stood up and felt for his keys in his jacket pocket, as he had a habit of doing. Reassuringly they were there, along with a complimentary travel-sized toothpaste.

"Odd?" he thought. He was right about Miss Welsh's sense of humour.

On his way home, Keith dropped into a newsagent's and bought a packet of chocolate buttons to take the strange taste away from his mouth, but otherwise his evening progressed fairly normally.

Later that night, relaxing in front of the TV sipping his tea, he started to feel some discomfort in his mouth as the pain relief wore off ... he felt around with his tongue and knew something wasn't quite right. So he crossed the hall, clicked on the bathroom light and grinned into the mirror for a closer inspection.

"Oh no!" he thought "it's a bloody hole!" feeling it with his finger.

"No wonder it's been a bit sensitive ... and that gum doesn't look too healthy ..." he noticed, lifting his top lip.

"Better give the dentist a ring ...".

Action Replay

With a rustle, Bob's leather glove rolled out of his hand and onto the path, ending up at the base of a low, crumbling brick wall, just to the side of his parked motorbike. Bob picked it up and put it in his helmet along with his phone, having just taken some photos of the bikes outside the Silver Ball Café, the cloudless blue sky forming a perfect backdrop for the ribbon of road curling into the distance. "The warmest December since records began" had tempted Bob and PJ onto the roads for a ride-out for a coffee, and it seemed every other motorcyclist in the county had had the same thought, the café full of like-minded leathery souls, all happily chatting over their steaming brews.

"What do you think of that new Ducati?"

"It's definitely global warming ..."

"How long is that breakfast going to be?"

"*Since records began?!* They only started in 1914!"

"I wish I'd got two eggs now ..."

The range of conversation that could be overheard was inspiring.

"Hello Bob" smiled Denise the waitress "here's your breakfast!"

"Ah, you get a beautifully served breakfast in here PJ, so you do" replied Bob in a false Irish accent, for no particular reason.

The cobwebs of another inactive, over-indulgent Christmas successfully blown away, Bob arrived home, settled in front of the TV and absent-mindedly started flicking through the photos on his phone ... they were good, but one looked odd.

"What's that?" It looked like a glove ...

"A video?" he noticed.

Curious, Bob hit the play symbol … With a rustle, a leather glove rolled out of his hand and onto the path, ending palm-up at the base of a low brick wall, just to the side of his parked bike. Bob smiled and hit the play symbol on his phone again. Down rolled the glove again ending palm-up, one finger pointing, next to the colourful purple radiator hose to the side of his bike. A full three seconds of footage! Of course, he'd hit the "video" button accidentally and inadvertently captured his falling glove for posterity! He pressed the play button again and with each roll of the glove, this delightfully insignificant moment in time appealed to his sense of humour more.

"Ridiculous! The boys will love it" he thought.

Smiling, Bob tapped out the title of his email *"Arty Bike Video"* and attached the video footage, along with the comment. "I've called it "The Descent of the Glove"—I hope you enjoy it"

Predictably, his friends' soon joined in the fun …

"That is *so* thought provoking! Why was the glove dropped? Was it ever retrieved? Would it have made the same sound if you hadn't been there? What damaged the wall? Will it be repaired? What is love anyway? How do we define happiness?"

PJ soon chipped in:

"It really resonates with me, the tumbling of the glove bringing into question the futility of the human condition. The broken wall signifying the walls we build around ourselves for protection. Or is it a metaphor for the crumbling of civilisation along with traditional social orders and norms? The juxtaposition of the vulgar purple radiator hoses, perhaps representing man's struggle to tame nature and his pursuit of the synthetic …"

Laughing, Bob replied "You are all correct in your incisive interpretations—I *did* mean to say all those things, and less. I thought I may have been wasting my time with my film career but you have reinvigorated my cinematic exploration of the movement of leather handwear for years to come. Thank you!"

For a spell, the accidental video took on almost legendary status (at least to Bob) and, for closer friends who shared his sense of humour, he would repeatedly show or send the video to reinforce its ludicrousness. Unfortunately, Bob's sense of humour was such that this would never *not* be funny. Long after, others had stopped laughing and dismissed it as a childish jape, Bob would still be giggling. A blessing and a curse ... and perhaps one of the reasons he lived on his own.

His repeated watching of the video became quite mesmeric, relaxing in a way, like a Tibetan monk chanting. With a cup of tea and a Christmas cake, for no reason at all, he repeatedly played the clip. The glove's movement was odd ... a definite roll rather than a drop, rather like a dung beetle curling into a ball and rolling down a sand dune. He started to examine the footage more closely ... the crumbling red brick wall with the occasional white faced brick, the rough, pot-holed tarmac, the bright purple of the radiator hose, the pointed finger of the glove at rest ... the sparkle of light by the finger ...

"Odd" he thought, he hadn't noticed that before.

"Wonder if I can zoom in?" but Bob lacked the technological know-how.

It was a definite glint in the sun ... easy to miss but, once you'd noticed it, impossible to ignore. As he played it a couple more times, he was more and more intrigued.

"What the hell is it?!" Looking outside he saw the weather was still good and the thought of riding back to take a closer look crossed his impetuous mind.

"Why not?! It's a good day! Any excuse for a ride!" he thought.

He got on the phone to PJ.

"Hello! Long time, no speak!" and Bob explained the situation.

"Sorry mate, I've said I'd go to the sales with Gemma"

Bob understood that PJ had commitments, so he set out on his own. Which wasn't a problem. He enjoyed his own company.

The café was closed from 1.30 pm so he had the pick of the spaces in the large car park, but he was only heading for one, the one right at the front, next to the crumbling brick wall. Alone in the car park he parked in exactly the same spot as he had previously, recognising the detail of the wall and the path.

"Yes, this is it!"

Looking down, he couldn't see anything unusual, just a path ... so, checking there was still no-one about, he got down on his hands and knees for a closer look, and there it was ... What looked like a small piece of glass was embedded in the tarmac path. He put on his reading glasses and had a closer look . . . no, it was the top of a ring! It looked like someone had dropped a ring and trodden it into the tarmac.

Carefully, he picked it out of the path with his key and it came free quite easily . . .

"Looks valuable" he thought, "someone will have missed this."

He decided to phone the café the following morning to ask if anyone had reported a ring missing. The thought did cross his mind someone might say "Yes" and pocket the ring themselves, but he knew Denise and the people behind the counter pretty well and they seemed honest to him.

"No, I've checked with the others and we haven't heard anything" came the reply from Denise over the phone. "OK thank you" Bob replied, pleased their honesty had been confirmed.

Bob had also thought he might keep the ring but it really did look valuable and, being an honest sort himself, he resolved to hand it in as lost property to the Police.

"Rest assured it will be safe with us" assured the desk Sergeant at the Station.

"I'd hope so!" Bob thought as he said his goodbyes, thinking he was never destined to be rich.

"You're a soft touch Bob, you really are!" laughed PJ when Bob explained what had happened. "I bet the copper has pocketed it!"

"Just the way I am!" replied Bob, " . . . poor and stupid!"

Over the coming week, Bob found himself watching the video again a couple of times, he just couldn't pass it in his photos without pressing play and smiling.

The unseasonably warm weather continued and the following weekend, PJ called Bob. "Fancy another run to the Silver Ball? We'll go a different route to make a change . . . never know you might find some more jewellery to give away!"

"Yes, highly amusing!" smiled Bob.

It was quite busy when they arrived but there was space at the front, including *that* space . . . so they pulled in. Bob looked down, expecting to see the indentation of the ring in the tarmac but instead something glinted in the sun . . . He kneeled down and what he saw stopped him breathing . . . exactly the same looking piece of glass in the same spot! Looking around, he eased it out again with his motorcycle key and . . .

"No way!" he said under his breath.

"What?" said PJ walking over.

"It's another damned ring!"

"Ha, ha! Nice one! Of course it is!" laughed PJ, spotting a wind-up when he saw one. "Let's have a look!"

"I'm telling you, it looks the same as the last one!"

"Seriously, stop winding me up! You know you put it there! You got me!"

"I swear on my mother's life it's true!"

"Your Mum died four years ago!"

"I'm telling the truth damn it" and there was something in the tone of Bob's voice that told PJ that he was. There it was, an identical diamond ring, glinting in the sun.

"What the hell is going on?" Bob sat on his sofa and gazed at the ring after he had cleaned it a little. It was identical in every way.

"What to do? . . ."

This time he thought he'd get it valued at the jewellers in town, so he took it down there the next day.

"It's a nice piece sir . . . are you thinking of selling it?"

"Not right now, I'm just trying to get an idea of value"

"Did it belong to a relative sir?

"Ahh, no, just something I picked up recently at a boot sale" Bob wasn't averse to the odd white lie.

"Well I think you have done very well" said the jeweller, peering up over his eyepiece "I'd give you £3000 now"

"What!" said Bob, blowing his cool cover.

"It's a *beautiful* ring and a good quality diamond . . . you let me know when you want to sell it now!"

"I will" Bob replied in shock.

"What the hell is going on?" he asked himself on his way home, pleased but confused. The same ring, in exactly the same spot . . . it just didn't make sense.

"It's obvious!" said PJ over the phone "What you've got there is a magic video! Each time you play it, like magic there's another ring!"

"Yes, very funny!" PJ was wailing with laughter at the end of the phone.

"What's going on, PJ?" Bob was starting to be concerned.

"I don't know! Just sell the bloody ring!"

"I might well do that! We'll split the money"

"It's *your* video, Bob!"

"No, I wouldn't have been there without you, we'll split it"

"Well, if you insist!".

After signing-off, Bob chuckled to himself "A magic video!"

He knew it was ridiculous but he couldn't get the thought out of his head.

He watched the video again, and there was the sparkle on the path . . .

"Is it possible?"

"Is it perhaps worth checking?"

Impulsively, Bob phoned PJ back.

"I'm going back to the café now, do you want to come?"

"What?! It's dark!" PJ said hesitantly.

"Go on then, but Gemma's expecting me back later so I can't be too long"

So back they went.

"I'm worried about you Bob . . ." PJ said walking over to the spot, "what do you think we are going to bloody see"

"I know, I know. Just let me check it out, and I maybe I can get some sleep!

"Get the torch up on your phone"

Bob knew exactly where to look now.

"Hold that torch still!"

"There's another one!" And there it was, identical to the others. They both stood up speechless staring at the ring in the the torchlight.

"I've got it!" said PJ, "It's a bloody test! They've put it there and they're watching us on CCTV now!"

"Now who's being stupid?! Just hold that torch still on the path!" replied Bob

"I'm going to play it again, just look at the spot"

They both crouched down and, as Bob hit the play button and the glove rustled to the ground, another ring appeared in the indentation.

"You are kidding me!" Bob eased the ring out of the path and hit the play button again. Another ring appeared!

"You're freaking me out now! What the hell is this" said PJ.

"I don't know but let's try it a few more times!"

"OK. I'd better phone Gemma" smiled PJ "looks like I'm going to be late!"

So the two friends carried on, crouched down beside the low wall, the mist of their breath illuminated by the torchlight, replaying the video and picking rings out of the tarmac path.

"You play and I'll pick them out" suggested PJ.

Play, pick, play, pick, play, pick … they got into a rhythm, and a pile of rings built up on the path.

"What the hell is this?!" beamed PJ. They couldn't believe their luck.

"I had one valued you know" said Bob, "Three grand each!"

PJ stopped.

"Now you *are* winding me up!

"Honestly" said Bob, "Three thousand *each*!"

PJ had a renewed focus and the speed of picking increased. Heads down, they got into a rhythm … play, pick, play, pick … for the most part with nothing being said. The odd vehicle would drive past but, behind the wall, they didn't attract too much attention. Until eventually, a van pulled into the car park.

"Hide the torch!" panicked Bob.

They scooped up the pile of rings and put them in PJ's deep jacket pockets.

"Stay calm, if anyone comes over we were looking for our keys" suggested PJ. They didn't. After five minutes, much to Bob's relief, the van pulled away.

"I'm not cut out for this cloak and dagger stuff!" sighed Bob "doesn't feel right sneaking around in the shado.."

PJ interrupted Bob by hitting him hard across the face with his helmet, sending him sprawling unconscious across the tarmac. It was a spur of the moment thing. In two hours, they had picked sixty-six rings out of the path … just under £200,000 and, for PJ, the price of their friendship had been reached.

Bob lay unconscious on the cold path and only became conscious of the gravel against his cheek fifteen minutes later. Groggy, he tried to pull himself up but he stumbled and fell against his bike. Another van driver then pulled in and noticed he was in difficulty.

"Are you alright mate?" he called over.

"Err, I don't know, no not really". He wasn't making much sense.

"There's no way you're riding that" said the van driver "Come and sit in here and I'll phone for an ambulance" Reluctantly, Bob agreed that was probably a good idea.

"You're going to be fine but we'd like to keep you in for observation for tonight and tomorrow" said the doctor at the hospital.

"Fine. Thank you" Bob replied distantly. He was still in shock. He had known PJ since they were at school together, OK not bosom buddies, but close enough. Resting back on his pillow, suddenly a thought occurred to him

"The phone!"

Urgently, he reached over to the chair by his bed for his jacket pocket ... as if he was quicker, the phone would be more likely to be there. He could feel it in the zipped pocket!

"Thank God! The bloody idiot didn't even have the sense to steal it!"

But as he pulled it out of the pocket his face dropped.

"Oh no!" the screen was splintered and the whole thing had obviously taken a heavy knock.

"Work, work! ..." Bob willed, pressing the buttons, but no matter how many times he tried, it wouldn't switch on.

Of course he tried to get it repaired but the phone just wouldn't start up. He got several people to try to recover the data, but they all told him it wasn't recoverable. The video was lost. He'd been meaning to back it up too but just hadn't got round to it.

Bob never saw or heard from PJ or Gemma again. He decided not to go to the Police, thinking that the chances of them believing a story about a magic video were slim. He had nothing to show them and would just look like an idiot. Which is exactly how he felt.

"Fuck them" he thought.

He tried to contact PJ but had no success, although, out of pure curiosity, Bob found him on Facebook a few months later. Gemma had left him, apparently. Sounded like he was doing OK, house, cars ... In honesty, Bob didn't care whether he was alive or dead.

Over the next few weeks he revisited the café and, although the breakfast was good and it was always good to see Denise, he never found another ring. Feeling foolish, he even tried to re-shoot a video of the falling glove, but to no avail.

Six months later, Bob took another summer ride out to the Café. It was a beautiful day but unusually quiet.

"Hi Denise, how are you?" he smiled as he approached the counter.

"Hello Bob, I'm fine thank you, how about you?"

"I'm good. Can I have a full English please?"

"Of course, I'll bring it over"

Denise always had a smile for Bob and he'd noticed lately that he would always get an extra egg on his plate. He knew she was single. Quiet. Unusual. He liked her. And, as she approached his table with his breakfast, he resolved to ask her something he had been meaning to for some time.

"So, if I asked you to come to dinner with me tonight, would you say no?" Bob asked as Denise put his plate down.

"No" Denise smiled back.

"Oh . . ." Bob was pleasantly surprised "..that's good"

"Have you got a car?" she said.

"Yes I have"

"Well pick me up in that at half seven!"

"I will, Denise. I will" smiled Bob.

As Denise walked away she turned back with a smile "I thought you'd never ask!"

As he walked out to his bike, the sun shining, the blue sky a perfect backdrop for the ribbon of road disappearing into the distance, his phone rang.

"Mr. Merton?"

"Yes. That's me"

"Police Service here sir. We're just getting back to you about the ring you dropped into us in December"

"Oh, yes" replied Bob, bad memories flooding back.

"Well, it hasn't been claimed and it now passes to your possession. So if you'd like to pick it up at some point sir?"

"Oh, thank you very much! I will" Bob's day was getting better and better!

Bob and Denise's date went very well. Well enough that, after three months, Bob plucked up the courage to propose to Denise at the café, on bended knee, in front of the whole breakfast crowd.

"You know I will!" she beamed.

On bended knee he opened the box, and Denise's eyes lit up at the sight of the ring.

"It's perfect!"

"Yes it is" said Bob.

Refinery

"Good morning sir!" Oscar prided himself on a level of customer service that that exceeded his customers' expectations.

"Good morning" replied the customer, impressed with Oscar's suit.

Oscar's hair was slicked back, his moustache small and hardly extending beyond his nostrils. The look was reminiscent of a notorious German dictator but this was completely at odds with his pleasant and professional demeanour.

"I wonder if you could recommend a suitable champagne for a special occasion?"

"Might I enquire as to the nature of the occasion?" said Oscar.

"Of course, my mother is receiving an award for her charity work in India. From the Viceroy no less" It was said with genuine pride but no boastfulness.

"Well!" Oscar beamed "congratulations are indeed in order! Let's see . . ."

He kept his best stock, at a higher level and stepped back to get a better look"

It was still dark outside and unusually quiet for 6.00am and Oscar relished the time to serve his customer properly.

"Well, we have a good selection of premium quality champagnes at the moment sir, ..."

"I'll be guided by you"

"Very well sir, let's see . . ." said Oscar scanning the choicest bottles.

"The irony is sir, I don't drink!" Oscar added.

"Just as well with all this temptation around you!"

"Quite sir" agreed Oscar "I did have a dalliance with the bottle in my youth and eventually decided that perhaps it was best appreciated from a distance".

The customer laughed politely.

"You know, I was thinking the Veuve Cliquot Premier Cru but I would thoroughly recommend this particular Tattinger Rose.... I think it's perfect for you"

"As I say, I will be guided by your good self"

"I appreciate the level of trust sir" beamed Oscar, as he carefully placed the bottle on the counter and started to wrap it in tissue.

"It's quiet in here this morning isn't it? commented the customer.

"I have to say, I like this time of the day sir" replied Oscar slipping the bottle into a beautiful presentation box, "although I fear the pace will soon pick up as the people of the town start to rise to greet the day!"

The customer was quite taken with Oscar's wistful, almost poetic demeanour his words seeming to hang in the air, reminiscent of a lost time.

Then, as rudely as a raspberry in a Carry On film, the main door buzzed in two tuneless tones announcing another customer's entrance through the sliding glass door. The moment was broken.

"Oh, and could I have a packet of polos and 20 Marlboro please" added the customer.

"Any petrol sir?" enquired Oscar

"Yes, number 6 please"

"Could I perhaps interest you in a Crème egg sir, three for a pound?" said Oscar, gesturing to the cardboard display tray on his counter. It was something Oscar had to ask but the customer could see it pained him.

"Ah no, that's fine thank you"

"Would you like a receipt for the entire transaction sir?" enquired Oscar.

"Yes, please"

Smiling, Oscar handed the customer his receipt, his box of champagne and vouchers for money off his next petrol purchase.

"And with that sir, I bid you good day"

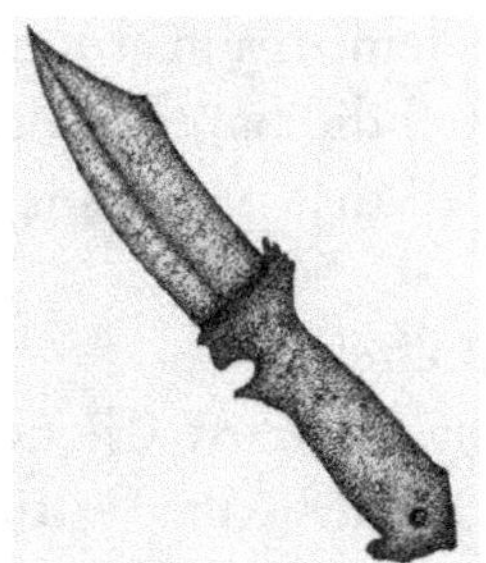

Your Parents would be Proud

Matt stood outside the entrance of the prison and took a long, clichéd look up at the blue sky streaked with high white cloud. He inhaled slow and long and he smiled. He was out! This time, it had been a relatively trouble-free stay at Her Majesty's pleasure, the Tai-Kwon-Do classes helping to establish him as someone who could handle himself and apart from the "prisoner stapling their scrotum to a workbench for a bet" incident, there wasn't much to write home about. Not that Matt ever did write home … he saw little point.

His parents lived in New Zealand but, despite their excellent postal service, he knew his letters, or any other correspondence for that matter, would not be opened. Their misgivings about their only son's career choice (robbery) was understandable and they had long since distanced themselves from him.

"You couldn't get any further away from me could you?!" Matt would say when they used to speak, although it really didn't bother him that much. He was always a loner, never much of a social animal and, to Matt, Christmas and birthdays were now much simpler.

This was his third stay in prison and, at twenty-seven, there was a growing realisation that perhaps his chosen career wasn't working out, to the point where thoughts of getting a "proper job" had even crossed his mind.

This perplexed him. He had always thought of himself as above that rat race. Although robbery was traditionally not a recipe for stability, in Matt's eyes it was head and shoulders above what he saw as the alternative…

"Everyone scurrying about, struggling to own their own brick box" Matt was fond of saying…"only to pass it on to their children who, through guilt would scurry about to buy their *own* brick box!". He knew even his parents' brick box in New Zealand would probably come to him eventually, although it was looking increasingly likely they'd leave it to a dog's home.

"But how would you feel, if *you'd* been robbed?" his parents used to ask, but with Matt, it wasn't personal. It was *corporate* fraud, moving money here, money there—*companies* not people, at least that's how he justified it.

"I wouldn't dream of knocking an old lady down for her purse!" he'd say. "Anyway, how many would I need to knock down for £500,000! There's no need for me to get my hands dirty!"

Matt had some funds, enough to rent somewhere and get used to life outside. He found a flat just north of London where the prices were kinder and he figured he might be able to stretch his rent to around two years there, maybe three. He didn't need to be in London anyway, all he needed was a good internet connection and somewhere quiet where he could concentrate and apply his particular gift…being able to analyse accounts and identify patterns that weren't apparent to most. But an "Achilles heel" had tripped him up in the past…in the euphoria of embezzlement, he'd get over-excited and tend to overlook the importance of covering his tracks. He'd get a little sloppy. One thing was for sure, he couldn't afford for another job to go wrong. Any goodwill he'd accrued between him and his "employer" had been well and truly exhausted by this last prison visit. Although there was little chance of the authorities ever linking Matt's employer to his incarceration, it reflected badly on them in financial embezzlement circles and Matt had already heard through the prison grapevine that "The Supervisor" wasn't happy. In reputational terms for "The Supervisor" it was only a flush of embarrassment at most, the slightest smear of egg on his face, but tolerance wasn't their forte and Matt knew it was only a matter of time until his phone rang. He'd changed his address, changed his mobile number, done all he could electronically to keep a distance, but at 6.15am on the Saturday, the inevitable call came.

"Hello?" said Matt half asleep.

"Matt! Ahh Matt . . . you're home! That's lovely! Settling in well I hope?" Matt's heart sank as the cultured tones of The Supervisor asked after his well-being.

"Not bad, thank you. Not bad"

"A lot more comfortable than your previous apartment, eh Matt?! It's the smell more than anything, they tell me"

"It's good to be out" said Matt matter-of-factly, knowing they had phoned for a reason and keen to dispense with the small-talk.

"Careless business, that last job, old boy"

"I know, I'm s . . . "

"Apologies! No time for those old boy! You know the score! We like to make progress not apologies!"

The phone line was dead for a moment.

"I c . . . "

"Dear Boy! We realise you are keen to make amends. *I* would be in your shoes . . . so we're giving you one last job"

"A last job?"

"Yes, to make amends, so to speak"

"I appreciate the opportunity but I really can't this time—I'm actually thinking of going straight".

"By all means think about it dear boy!" There was a silence.

"It's not going to happen, but by all means think about it!"

"No, I mean it"

"I'm sure you do but we couldn't possibly allow such a waste of talent! You're a trifle sloppy dear boy and *we* can't risk a direct connection with you any further of course, but we are *very* happy to allow other parties to use your services, for a small fee of course. After this job"

"And if I refuse?"

"Oh don't be like that Matt. By all means you can refuse, of course. We live in a free country dear boy. But with refusal comes consequences"

Matt was aware of what The Supervisor was capable of and he knew deep down that eventually, he would have to do this job.

"OK, what is it?"

"A robbery, dear boy"

"OK"

"A Mrs Greer"

"Mrs . . ."

"You don't know her" interrupted The Supervisor, "she lives at 34 Granville Gardens, NW6, she has two sons, five grandchildren, getting a little frail—worked hard all her life. A good person . . . we want you to rob her".

"That's not really my area" Matt pointed out nervously "You know it isn't".

"Quite" replied The Supervisor. "It'll make a change"

"Is she rich?" Matt asked, not knowing why he had.

"No, not at all, draws a pension"

"So why?"

"Amusement, I suppose. Oh and we want you to really hurt her in the process"

"What?!"

"I'd like you to hurt her badly dear boy"

"But why?" Matt asked with growing concern.

"Because we say so"

"But it's pointless!"

"Financially yes, but it entertains me . . . and your parents will suffer if you don't do it"

"What!?" I won't do it!"

"Perfectly fair old boy, it's your decision" The Supervisor said perkily and put the phone down.

"Shit!" thought Matt. There was no way of contacting The Supervisor, it was always Matt that got the call. He paced around the living room for a full ten minutes, the words "Want you to hurt her" circulating in his head.

"Phone back, phone back" he begged to himself . . . but there was no call.

Five nervous hours later, there was still no call.

A message pinged through on his computer. Matt didn't recognise the sender and was about to delete it but the photographs caught his eye.

"House fire in New Zealand" was the title. The whole place was ablaze . . . believed to be an electrical fault . . . couple didn't stand a chance.

In panic, Matt ran for his phone, his parent's number was in there somewhere. "There!"

He dialled frantically.

"Hello" answered a frail female voice.

"Mum is that you?!" Matt shouted down the phone.

"Matt!" his mother blurted, and started to cry.

"Are you alright Mum?"

"Not really" she wobbled "our neighbours have had a terrible fire and we're being told there were two people in there. We don't think they made it". His mother sobbed.

"Are *you* alright though? Your house wasn't affected?"

"No, no we're fine. It's the shock of it all" his mother sobbed, "Poor Fran and Jack. We can't believe it"

Matt couldn't believe it either.

An hour later, came the call that Matt was waiting for.

"Dear boy!"

"Was that you?!" asked Matt.

"Was what me?" replied the Supervisor innocently.

"You know what! The house fire!"

"Sorry dear boy, I have trouble keeping up with news here, let alone that in New Zealand!"

"How do you know my parents are in New Zealand?!"

"Matt, Matt... its not that difficult these days you know! The world's a lot smaller, a *lot* smaller—you'd be surprised!"

"Have you thought about our proposal?" said the Supervisor.

"Yes"

"Splendid, so you'll do it?"

"No, I can't—why should she suffer?"

"Why should *anyone* suffer?" replied the Supervisor, "It's a good question, but people do, don't they... the Lord moves in mysterious ways"

"But why *her*?"

"Oh, a *conscience*! Who'd have thought it?!" laughed the Supervisor.

"But it could be *your* mother" pointed out Matt.

"Oh and empathy too!" The Supervisor roared "It wouldn't be *mine*—I wouldn't want to mess with her! Look, we both know you're going to do the job because you have no choice—it's just a bit of fun"

"But I can't" said Matt with real desparation in his voice.

"OK" came the same perky voice.

"NOO!" Matt interrrupted quickly "OK. OK, I'll do it"

"A very sensible decision Matt. Shall we say tomorrow?"

"Now just to clarify, when we said really hurt her, we meant kill of course"

"No . . ."

"No guns, with your hands dear boy, *with your hands!*" and the phone went dead.

That night, sleep didn't come easily to Matt. He replayed the conversation with The Supervisor in his head a hundred times, tried to figure a way out, but he knew there was no way. No running, no contacting the Police, no choice . . .

He had to kill Mrs Greer or his parents would be killed.

At precisely 9.00am that morning, his computer pinged the receipt of a message. It was in a font that looked like newspaper print cut up to make words, like an electronic kidnap ransom note. It read "At 3.00pm today, she'll be walking to her bowls club. Time to get your hands dirty!" As it closed, the message deleted. He knew it was untraceable and he knew what he had to do at three o'clock.

He paced up and down his flat for hours.

"It's got to be quick, painless . . . " He had to kill her, but *how?*

"Approach her from behind in a quiet part of her route, don't have to face her . . . yes, there's a place . . . twist her neck quickly" He had learned something of such techniques reading around his Tae Kwon Do.

Yes, that was the way, if he got it right it would be instant. *If* he got it right . . .

"Shit! There's just one chance! Got to be committed, no hesitation, no messing . . . "

He burst into tears, but he knew there was no choice. He thought about her two sons, her five grandchildren. But his parents *would* be killed. He had to kill her, it was as simple as that.

What would he do afterwards?

"Take off, get across to Europe, slate wiped clean . . . a new start. Maybe get to New Zealand? Maybe . . . "

The alarm sounded, it was 2.30. Time to make his way across town.

It was a lovely afternoon and he walked briskly with a steely determination.

He passed several people but didn't see any of them, looking straight ahead, replaying what he was going to do in his mind.

"Don't think, just focus, and do it . . ."

His heart pounded, he couldn't get the thought of her sons out of his mind. He was about to kill their mother.

"Focus for Christ's sake, or it'll be *your* mother!" the voice screamed in his head.

2.50 . . . he was at the edge of the park across from Granville Gardens and he could see the front door of number 34. It was terraced, so she should come out that way to walk to the bowls club just off that road.

"Maybe she'll slip out the back!" he panicked. "No, no she should come out the front . . . " the voice in his head reassured him.

The door opened and, her straw bag hanging over her arm and green scarf wrapped over her head, Mrs Greer left her house.

She was exactly as The Supervisor had described.

"Shit!". Matt moved from the park to cross the road and, at a distance, turned round to follow her. It was quiet, just before the roads filled with parents collecting their children from school. Matt slowed his step to keep a safe distance. His heart pounded and the birds singing in the tree-lined road was deafening. He knew she would turn off to the club soon . . . She turned into the back street . . . not a soul, only the birds singing, as if they knew what was about to happen.

"Now!" he thought "Now!". Breathing quick and shallow Matt quickened his step . . . close enough to smell her perfume, he raised his arms to her neck. But Mrs Greer dropped down and turned towards him, as quick as

he'd seen anyone move. Before he could blink, the knife had entered Matt's belly just under his breast bone and Mrs Greer had pulled it up into his diaphragm with a force that belied her years.

"Sorry dear boy" she said, as Matt hung on the knife. He was in shock, eyes wide as The Supervisor dragged him into the bushes, quickly losing consciousness, a loud buzzing in his head taking over from the cacophony of bird song. He urgently pulled himself up to the Supervisor's ear.

"My parents?!"

"Perfectly fine. They would be proud of you. Now rest dear boy, rest" the Supervisor said, laying him gently on the ground.

And Matt slipped away, for the first time feeling at peace, all around the birds singing.

Battery Farming

"What are those Dad?" asked Joe from the back of the car.

"What are what?"

"Those blue things in the field?"

"Ahh" replied Andrew, his father.

"They're solar panels. The sun shines on them and they make electricity"

"Ohh . . ." said Joe deep in thought as the sun streamed through the car window. It was a large field and it was full of neat rows of large blue panels, as far as you could see, all looking up in unison towards the sun, as if following its downward arc at the end of the afternoon.

"But why do those sheep need solar panels?" asked Joe.

In amongst the panels, sheep were grazing contentedly, apparently happy to share their field with the new technology.

Andrew smiled and saw an opportunity for some fun.

"Well the sheep need electricity too you know" he said.

"No they don't!" replied Joe, quite an astute child.

"Well how are they going to make a cup of tea then?" asked his father.

"Ha!" Joe laughed "Sheep don't drink tea!"

"Not all of them, no, some prefer coffee, but they've got to boil the kettle haven't they?"

"They don't drink tea *or* coffee! Just water from a trough!"

"Oh years ago, yes" Andrew replied "but they've moved on now. Now they've got the solar panels they love nothing better than a nice cup of tea when they put their feet up at the end of the day"

"*Feet!*" Joe protested, "Sheep don't have feet!"

"Ok, you've got me there . . . put their hooves up then!"

"Dad, you can be very silly you know" said Joe in a serious tone that reminded Andrew of his wife.

"Look you asked me what they were for and I'm telling you!"

Their drive continued down the country lane route to Andrew's sister's house, their electric car whispering through the villages, only road noise audible in the cabin. It was going to take another hour or more and Andrew thought a bit more nonsense may pass the time. "Of course, the sheep grow them from seeds you know"

"What?" replied Joe, distracted.

"Those solar panels, they grow them from seeds" said Andrew waiting for a reaction.

"No they don't! Men put them there!"

"I'm telling you" smiled Andrew "the sheep buy the packets of seeds from the garden centre! They're tiny little blue squares but if they're looked after, and watered regularly, they grow into nice big blue panels like you saw!"

"I don't think you are telling the truth" said Joe, with a wobble in his voice that suggested that maybe they actually *did* grow them from seeds.

"Honestly! They planted them in lovely neat rows too, didn't they"

"You *know* they didn't Dad" pointed out Joe. He was getting too smart to fool these days and, even at seven, Andrew thought he'd probably go far.

"I didn't hear you pull up in that thing!" said his sister Mandy, opening her door to Andrew.

"Yeah, it's quiet alright, and it holds its charge for two weeks! I kind of miss the exhaust noise though".

Mandy had no urge to continue discussing the car. "It's really good of you to come over" she said pecking him on the cheek, "I can't put this wardrobe together for the life of me"

"No problem Sis" Andrew's wife was away at a work conference and it gave him and his son something to do.

"Any chance of a cuppa?" asked Andrew as he leafed through the instructions.

"Yes" laughed Joe "like the sheep!"

"The sheep?" asked Mandy.

"Yes, Dad says the sheep drink tea but I don't believe him!"

Andrew looked up and smiled.

"He said they *need* electricity?!"

"Well, if Dad says it then it must be true" she smiled.

Against all the odds, the wardrobe went together as per the instructions and Mandy was delighted.

"I owe you brother"

"Always" smiled Andrew, kissing her goodbye.

It was dark by the time they left and their return drive took them past the solar panel field, softly lit by some security lighting.

"I can't see any sheep now" said Joe.

The devilment rising again, Andrew replied.

"Well, you won't see them at night . . ."

"Why?" replied Joe.

"Well, they've got a big games room under the field"

"What?"

"Oh yes, television, pool tables, table tennis, it's amazing! They love to have a play before they go to bed, just like you"

"Ha ha!" laughed Joe, so hard that bubbles came out of his nose.

Back in the field, the sheep were all gathered at the far end in a perfect line, their fleeces bright in the glow of the security lighting.

The "farmer" walked across to the head of the queue and pressed the button.

"Down you go then my beauties" he said as a large section of grass slowly rose to reveal a shallow concrete slope down into an underground room.

The sheep all started to walk at once, each in perfect step, they marched down the ramp and stood in front of the ten charging bays, behind the other robotic sheep that had been charging during the day.

"Time for a top-up" said the "farmer" pressing a button to release the charged sheep from their foot charging connections. "Come on, let these have a go now" he said and the charged sheep all took five steps back in unison.

The "farmer" smiled. He had made a lot of money from the solar panels. The disease outbreak of 2032 had been devastating for his flock. The worms had eaten the sheep from the inside and he'd managed their suffering as best he could, but he couldn't face something like that happening again. However, after a time, he found he really missed his sheep and the routines of the land . . . His cousin had come up with the idea, along with the random programming for the day . . . you really couldn't tell them from the real thing! He said he might work on some cows next, but that would take some time.

"That's it my beauties!" the "farmer" smiled as he switched on their over-night charger, "It's going to be another lovely sunny day tomorrow".

The Chronicles of Vlad

1. Vlad the Indifferent

"I've really got no strong feelings either way" said Vlad the Indifferent, eyes rolling as his brother presented his latest victim on a spike.

"*No strong feelings?!* Look it goes *right through him!*" pointed out Vlad, pointedly.

"Yeah" dismissed Vlad, "just like all the others."

"Exactly! Just like all the rest! You don't get to be called *Vlad the Impaler* without it going all the way through and out the other side!"

"S'pose you're right" said Vlad indifferently "you'd be called Vlad the Poker otherwise".

"Exactly, and I'm not! I'm called *Vlad the Impaler!*"

"Yes I think we've established that" replied Vlad the Indifferent.

"You are *so* bloody..." fumed Vlad the Impaler leaning his spiked victim against the wall, "so bloody... *indifferent!*"

"Am I?"

"Yes, I have to say that after all these years, I have noticed that you definitely are!"

"If you say so" Vlad replied, not looking up from his paper.

"I'll come back from a hard days impaling and do you show *any* interest or enthusiasm at all? *No, you do not!* Sometimes I don't know why I bother!"

"Beats me" said Vlad, turning the page.

"Well I bother because I'm *Vlad the Impaler* and if I didn't impale people . . . "

"You'd just be called Vlad?" Vlad interrupted.

"Yes! I'd just be called Vlad! Is that what you want?!"

"Yeah, why not" Vlad replied without looking up.

"Why not?! *Why not?!*" Vlad replied in shock. "Well for one thing, it would be hard to sort out our post wouldn't it"

"No, I'd still be Vlad the Indifferent" Vlad said indifferently.

"AND!" Vlad the Impaler quickly added, "Who else is going to keep the population numbers down?"

"I don't know" replied Vlad, "Vlad the Sniper?"

"Don't be ridiculous! You know he's in Afghanistan and very happy there"

"Whatever" said Vlad.

"This has always been your problem hasn't it"

"Has it?" replied Vlad, head still in the newspaper.

"Yes it *really* has! Your complete lack of opinion on bloody anything!"

"Maybe" said Vlad.

"No, not maybe. *Definitely!*"

"If you say so" said Vlad.

"Well, I've had enough!"

"That's nice . . . " said Vlad, still engrossed in the article.

"No *really*" said Vlad the Impaler, one foot on his victim, withdrawing the spike. "I've had *enough!*" And Vlad thrust his spike through the newspaper and into Vlad's chest . . . straight through and out the other side. Vlad the Indifferent looked up from his paper and, with one hand on the spike, looked his impaler straight in the eye.

"Don't you think for one moment that I might be a *little tired* of your *constant impaling?*"

"*Really?*" said Vlad, excited at the prospect of an opinion forming.

"Nah" said Vlad "I can take it or leave it".

2. Vlad the Inhaler

"But you just breathed *out!*" shouted Vlad the Impaler.

"Yes" pointed out Vlad the Inhaler, stating the obvious.

"But you're Vlad the *Inhaler!*"

"Yes!" Vlad repeated "but I need to breathe!"

"Do you?"

"Well, technically no, I don't, I'm undead as you know, but it just gets uncomfortable"

"What you just balloon up?"

"Exactly . . . and it really doesn't help with my flatulence"

"So why do they call you Vlad the Inhaler cousin?"

"It's the asthma" wheezed Vlad, shaking his inhaler.

"Oh that can't be much fun" said Vlad the Impaler.

Vlad the Inhaler put his inhaler between his fangs and inhaled sharply.

"Noo . . . . it's nooot" he wheezed, exhaling.

"I imagine the wheeziness undermines you a little when you're making threats?" said Vlad the Impaler.

"It really does" Vlad nodded "it's starting to get in the way . . . that's why I called you".

"Well if I can help cousin, I'd be pleased to, but what you suggested over the phone sounds a little extreme"

"No, no" wheezed Vlad, "I've thought it through and it'll be fine. I'm undead after all"

"Well, if you're sure" said Vlad sharpening his spike "It's going to smart a bit though".

"Just do it!" wheezed Vlad impatiently.

Vlad the Impaler nodded. "Very well cousin", and then repeatedly thrust his spike into Vlad the Inhaler's chest . . . In, out, in, out . . . he circled Vlad as he thrust, liberally perforating his chest.

Vlad the Inhaler sat there with tears running down his cheeks.

"Would you like a tissue?" offered Vlad the Impaler.

"Thank you" said Vlad pulling some from the box to wipe away the tears.

"Do you know what . . ." said Vlad the Inhaler, "my chest has never felt so free!" He inhaled and exhaled deeply, no hint of a wheeze, sucking a tissue onto his chest, such was the free movement of air. "I can't thank you enough cousin!".

"It's my pleasure" replied Vlad the Impaler "it's good to see such gratitude after an impaling!"

"Well I won't be needing this anymore!" smiled Vlad, tossing his inhaler into the bin.

"But what shall we call you now cousin?" asked Vlad the Impaler.

"Vlad?" suggested Vlad.

"Yes!" smiled Vlad the Impaler. "From this day forth, you shall be known simply as *Vlad!*"

3. *Vlad the Upholsterer*

"Damn it!" cursed Vlad the Impaler, as he accidentally drew his sharp spike across his new sofa, opening up the cushion like the belly of a cow. He tried pushing the stuffing back in and turning it over but he knew it was there and realised it was only a matter of time before he'd need to call his friend.

He flicked through his phone contacts "Vlad the Aviator . . . Vlad the Translator . . ." Eventually he found him "Ahh! Vlad the Upholsterer!" and he dialled the number.

"Hello, Vlad the Upholsterer, how may I help you?" came the professional reply.

"Vlad, it's me. Vlad the Impaler"

"Oh, hello Vlad" replied Vlad with a cautious note in his voice, "it's been quite a while"

"It has, it has" replied Vlad "I'm sorry, I should have called but, you know how it is, time flies when you're having fun!"

"Well, actually I've only just got back to work" replied Vlad.

"Ah good. You're back! That's splendid news, I have a job for you"

"Err . . . I'm not sure Vlad" he hesitated.

"*What?*" asked Vlad the Impaler innocently.

"You know very well what!" said Vlad.

"Oh *that!* It wasn't personal, it's just what I do!"

"I understand that but after you impaled me and kept me off work for six months, you can understand why I'm slightly hesitant"

"You've got to learn to let these things go Vlad, they can make you ill" said Vlad the Impaler "OK, if I promise *not* to impale you or anyone else during your visit, will you help me?"

"Well say it then?" insisted Vlad.

"OK, *I promise!*"

"Promise *what?*"

"OK, *I promise not to impale you at all!*"

"*Really* promise?" insisted Vlad the Upholsterer.

"Of course!" snapped Vlad "I want this blessed sofa fixed!"

"OK, I'll be round at three"

"Perfect!" replied Vlad the Impaler, "I'll have the kettle on".

At 2.45, there were six loud knocks at Vlad the Impaler's door. "Strange . . ." thought Vlad, "he's always bang on time, never early, never late".

Vlad opened the door to find a man pinned to the outside of it. Vlad the Stapler had industrially stapled a victim to his front door for a joke! He could see his cape disappear round the corner as he ran off, and it wasn't the first time. "Grow up you idiot!" shouted Vlad the Impaler. He removed the groaning victim from the door, impaled him and threw him on the feature body-pile on his front lawn. "Bloody juvenile" he muttered.

At precisely three o'clock, Vlad the Upholsterer knocked at the door. "I see business has been good for you Vlad" said Vlad the Upholsterer glancing at the body pile and swallowing uncomfortably.

"Yes, quite brisk lately thank you" smiled Vlad "I can't complain, now come in."

Vlad felt uneasy as Vlad the Impaler closed the door behind him and led him into the small living room.

"The sofa looks fine!" said Vlad the Upholsterer nervously. Vlad the Impaler smiled and flipped the cushion over.

"Ah, I see. What happened?"

"Caught it with a spike" replied Vlad.

"Ah, that would do it". Vlad the Upholsterer's mouth was dry and he felt the room, close in on him a little. "I'll take it away with me. You'll have it back in a couple of days".

"I was hoping you could repair it now"

"It's a nasty tear that. Looks easy but it's going to take some time. Ready on Wednesday though" said Vlad keen to leave.

"Are you *absolutely sure* you can't repair it now?" asked Vlad the Impaler, reaching for his spike.

"Well, as you put it like that, I'll see what I can do shall I?!"

"I'd appreciate that" smiled Vlad, his favoured impaling arm returning to his side.

Vlad the Upholsterer laid out his tools and began his repair.

"Would you like a cup of tea?" offered Vlad, trying to make an effort.

"Yes please" replied Vlad feeling more at ease. After a few minutes, Vlad the Impaler returned with refreshments. As he went to put the tray down, he was stopped in his tracks by what he saw. "That's a big needle you have there" he said, his eyes lighting up.

"Yes" Vlad replied engrossed in his work, "you need a fairly big needle to get through the thick material"

"To . . . *impale* it, so to speak" said Vlad, eyes widening.

"Yes, you could say that" replied Vlad still engrossed in the detail of his work, not noticing Vlad reaching for the spike. Then suddenly the seriousness of his situation dawned on him. He looked up just as Vlad the Impaler thrust his spike into his chest—straight through his heart and out the other side.

Now the sofa was soaked in blood *as well as torn* . . .

"Damn!" cursed Vlad the Impaler.

4. Vlad the Impala

Vlad the Upholsterer could still feel the sharp pain in his chest from his cousin's spike as he woke up. But there was no spike. As he opened his eyes, he could feel an intense heat on his face and the dust of the Serengeti catching at the back of his throat. As he moved his arms to get up he knew something was amiss . . . no hands! He was shocked to see his arms were covered in a golden fur ending with black hooves! Instinctively he sprang up on all fours like Bambi and took a good look at himself . . . there was no doubt, he had come back as an antelope! And he had never felt so good! The constant ache in his back and neck from repairing soft furnishings was gone and there was no way he was going to hold a needle ever again! To say Vlad had a spring in his step was an understatement. He had never been so happy! He bounced around the plain with gay abandon, free as a bird, sucking in the warm air.

As the sun set, the sky alive with shimmering oranges and golds, the tall, willowy silhouette of a Masai warrior could be seen on the horizon. Motionless he stood there, absorbing his environment, patiently planning his hunt, his long spear vertical at his side. His eyes narrowed on the impala dancing on the plain below ... now was not the time ... tomorrow he would hunt. His red and white body paint seemed to glow in the evening sun and, across his chest a single word ...

"Vlad"

Raoul

"Goal!" screamed the commentator from the big screen that covered the wall at the back of the stage in the "Plough & Harrow".

The Tottenham fans hit the roof as the goal went in but Adam was non-plussed. He could take football or leave it and waiting for the game to finish was just getting in the way of him setting up his drum kit.

"We've got another twenty minutes yet and probably five more extra time on top of that!" he moaned in the direction of Dean the bass player.

"Relax and finish your drink man, there's plenty of time!" replied Dean, hoping that there was enough time for Tottenham to equalise. But Adam's attention span was famously short. "There's always something on here isn't there!" The small London pub was starting to get busy. Adam got out of his chair and started wandering about like a caged animal. It was true, the band never seemed to be able just to turn up, set up and play, there was always some delay.

He stared at the screen behind the stage and decided to put a few small bags of gear on the stage ready to unpack. He carefully ducked under the projected picture as he placed the bags on the stage. After bag number five, there was a collective groan from the customers . . . the game had ended and Tottenham had failed to equalise

"About time too" Adam muttered under his breath, relieved the screen would be raised so he could stop his "Hunchback of Notredame" impression.

On screen, the victorious Barcelona players were clapping the fans while the Tottenham players mostly sat down and looked bewildered.

"Look!" Adam called over to the lads in the band smiling as he raised his hand close to the screen. The Barcelona player known simply as Raoul was walking across the pitch towards the dressing room. Adam carefully positioned his hand so that Raoul's projected image appeared to walk onto it, and then moved his hand to follow his walk! Raoul appeared to be walking on Adam's hand! Dean saw this from across the bar and instantly splurted out his beer in an uncontrolled burst of laughter, some coming out of his nose.

Adam laughed and closed his hand on Raoul, pretending to put him in his jacket pocket, and turned away.

"Oh please stop!" Dean wheezed to himself, trying to control the grip of laughter until gradually it subsided and he could breathe again.

"Oh my God, that's the funniest thing I have *ever* seen" laughed Dean. Adam smiled "It wasn't *that* good!"

The gig went very well. They always did. Experienced musicians, a great band and an appreciative, slightly inebriated audience combined to produce a great evening. As Adam opened the rear door to the car park, the rush of cool autumn night air was welcome, but the prospect of dismantling the drum kit and the rest of the gear was not. "A necessary evil" they all thought, a small price to pay for such a good time. It was one of those evenings when getting paid for it was an added bonus—they would have all done it for nothing.

Adam's drive home was uneventful, pulling into his parking space outside his flat at half past two. It was late but tomorrow (actually today) was Saturday and he had nothing planned. He threw his jacket onto a chair in the living room, undressed and headed straight to bed.

"Has anyone seen Raoul?" shouted the Barcelona trainer down the coach.

"He said he had a flight to catch with his girlfriend . . . weekend in Italy wasn't it?" shouted Francini, the defender.

"Ah yes. You're right! He'll miss a good party!" A huge cheer went up on the coach, the team still high from their victory.

Raoul opened his eyes. It was dark and cool, as if he had woken up too early on a winter morning. He waited for his brain to engage and tell him where he was in those first few moments of consciousness, but it didn't.

In a mild panic he jerked himself into an upright position but it was difficult to stay there, surrounded by what felt like a soft material. "What is this?!" There was some light to his left so he crawled towards that, the material soft against his hands and bare knees, eventually crawling out of Adam's jacket pocket and standing in his Barcelona kit on top of the jacket on the arm of the chair.

"*What is this?*" he said out loud this time in shock.

"Must be dreaming . . ." he thought. He pinched his grass stained leg and felt the pain well enough . . . this was no dream.

Compounding his shock, just then the door of the living room opened and in walked a relatively huge, stark naked Adam, on his way to get a glass of water from the kitchen.

"Holy Mary Mother of God!" shouted Raoul, almost forgetting his size and location.

Adam heard the faint sound and instinctively covered his genitals with his hand "Who's there!" he said, on guard.

"Hey!" shouted Raoul at the top of his voice. Adam glanced over at the TV to see if it was on. It wasn't.

"*Hey!*" Raoul screamed. Adam jumped and switched the light on. And that's when he saw him, standing on the jacket.

"What the . . . ?!" Adam said to himself staring at the action figure-sized football character.

"Yes you! I am down here" shouted Raoul in his Spanish accent.

Adam stood there in shock, forgetting to cover his genitals any further.

Despite his relative size, Adam didn't come across to Raoul as a threat.

"What the fuck am I doing here?!" Raoul shouted "do you know anything about this?"

Adam shook his head and turned away and headed for his room, sleepily dismissing what he had seen. Still thirsty, he pulled on a pair of boxer shorts and headed back to the armchair.

"Yes I am still here!" shouted Raoul

"Jesus!" Adam stood there in shock.

"*You're* shocked?" asked Raoul, "How do you think *I* feel?!"

"*What has happened here?!*" shouted Raoul.

It was then that Adam noticed the number seven on his shirt. "You're Raoul!"

"Yes, thank you! I know who I am, I just don't know what is going on!"

"Stay there" said Adam, his thirst getting the better of him and he headed for the kitchen in a state of shock to get that glass of water.

"If you walk away again!" shouted a furious Raoul "I'll . . . ."

Unthreatened, Adam knelt by the sofa and tried to take the situation in. Then he remembered the game, the projected player on his hand . . .

"No way!" he said to himself.

"What did you say?"

"I think I know what might have happened here" said Adam, not believing that it possibly could. He was open-minded sort of chap but there was a limit.

"Could you give me some of that water please?" shouted Raoul, thirsty from his game.

"Of course" replied Adam, partially accepting his conversation with a footballer the size of his thumb. He dipped his finger in the glass and dropped a couple of drops near Raoul on the jacket. Raoul knelt down and pushed his hands into a droplet, rubbing them together and splashing some up into his face.

"Shit" shouted Raoul, standing up sharply.

"What?" asked Adam.

"I need to meet my girlfriend at the airport at three to fly to Italy"

"Hold on!" blurted Adam "I think the more pressing problem here is that you're in my living room and you're the size of a toy soldier!"

"You are right" agreed Raoul, "You said you think you know what might have happened?"

"Well maybe" said Adam, unsure that it was an explanation for what was before him. Adam explained the events of the night before.

"You *asshole!*" shouted Raoul, known for a fiery temperament.

"I didn't know you'd end up in my bloody pocket did I!" shouted Adam.

"Well you've got to get me back!"

Just then, an opportunistic thought crossed Adam's mind. "What would the paper's say? A miniature Raoul, transported from a projector screen . . . the publicity, the money!"

"Ehh, *asshole!*" shouted Raoul "*I said you've got to get me back!*"

"Yeah, yeah" replied Adam, running through the options in his head.

Kneeling in his boxer shorts, looking down at 2015's "Footballer of the Year" Adam smiled "This is amazing!"

The expression on Adam's face was one that Raoul had seen a few times on his way "up". It was the expression of someone who had seen an opportunity to make some money for themselves off the back of his fame.

"Ahhh, it is like that is it?!"

"Like what?" Adam said innocently.

"If it's about money, I can give you money!"

"What, no . . ." Adam replied too quickly, slightly ashamed.

"How much then?" asked Raoul.

"What?"

"How much? If you can get me back how much do you want?"

"If you can get me back soon, I'll give you five million euros. How is that sounding to you?"

"Five million euros! That's a good lottery win" Adam thought with a distant smile "A life changer!"

Then he caught sight of the slightly pathetic image of himself in the mirror kneeling in front of the armchair in his boxer shorts, overweight, thinking about extorting money from a tiny footballer . . . In a pang of conscience Adam replied "No keep your money, it's my fault you're here. I'll get you back somehow"

"Seriously my friend the money is not a problem, I just need to get back" Raoul replied, genuine concern creeping in. Then a thought occurred to him. "This bar you talk of, does it show a lot of football?"

"Yes, all the time"

"Even under twenty-one matches?"

"Probably the big teams, yes. Why?"

"Barca's under twenty-ones are playing at noon today!"

"Hold on that's eleven this morning our time" Adam pointed out, glancing at the clock on the living room cabinet. Adam checked his phone for the Sky Sports listings "Yes, it's on!" he smiled. "We've got two hours! Right, don't move, I'm getting some clothes on!"

"Thank the Lord for that" said Raoul. He went to look at his watch but just stared at a naked wrist.

"Stay where you are!" shouted Adam from his bedroom.

"I have no plans!" Raoul shouted. Things were getting more surreal by the minute.

"Can you eat something?" asked Adam.

It wasn't high on the list of Raoul's concerns but it had been a while. "Yes, I am a little hungry"

Adam cupped his hand and let Raoul walk onto it … *actually* walk onto it this time. He cupped his other hand around him, walked him across the room to the kitchen table and let him walk onto it.

It reminded Adam of the old TV series he used to like "Land of the Giants" where the crew of the spaceship landed on earth to find they were tiny relative to everything else. Breakfast spoons like shovels and cats like tigers, they spent their time hiding from the giant people. But Raoul had nothing to fear.

"Only got Rice Krispies I'm afraid" said Adam.

"It is fine" replied Raoul, used to taking a little more care with his diet. After the milk had soaked in a little, Adam carefully spooned two Rice Krispies out of his bowl and placed them on the place mat next to Raoul.

"Sorry, no spoon" said Adam.

"It is not a problem" replied Raoul, pulling pieces off with his hands.

They ate in silence, both in a state of suspended belief.

"Can I wash my hands?" asked Raoul.

"Oh, of course" replied Adam, tearing off a corner of paper towel, wetting it and leaving it beside Raoul.

They discussed how they were going to return Raoul to Barcelona and that, if he was away for much longer, it would be all over the news and social media.

"What is your name?" asked Raoul.

"Adam"

"It is good to meet you Adam, despite the circumstances being unusual".

Between them, they decided that the safest place for Raoul to travel in was back in his jacket pocket. So they left the house and drove back to the Plough and Harrow.

"Good!" said Adam as they pulled up outside, the poster in the pub window confirming that the game was being shown.

"Best you stay in there until the last moment I think" cautioned Adam.

"I think you are right" shouted Raoul.

"Hello again" said a young barman recognising Adam from the night before.

"Hello. Can I ask, is that the under 21's match showing now?"

"Yes, just about to start. I don't know why we bother. We only get a handful of people in for them, few Spaniards and oddballs. Can I get you a drink?"

"Half a bitter please" Adam wanted to keep a clear head.

"Can I have one!" shouted Raoul.

"Sorry, what was that" said the barman.

"Oh nothing, just talking to myself" replied Adam, opening his pocket and glaring at Raoul.

The preparations for the match were on the screen already. Players stretched, officials chatted and walked the line and the modest crowd waited in anticipation. It was a beautiful day in Barcelona, in contrast to the slightly gloomy day in London.

Adam walked over to the screen and put his half a bitter down on the table.

"OK, I think it's time" he said to Raoul.

"Yes, let's give it a try!" Raoul replied hopefully.

Adam looked around. Everyone was talking or reading the paper, no-one looking at the screen yet. He carefully gathered Raoul into his hand and then opened his palm, the footballer standing on it, still in his kit from the previous match.

"We'll try as we said" said Adam.

Raoul nodded nervously and instinctively started to limber up on Adam's palm, stretching and running in short bursts on the spot. Adam raised his palm to the screen until they touched.

"Just by the line, near the tunnel would be best" shouted Raoul.

Adam moved his hand and Raoul ran off it, into the image on the screen!

"My God!" said Adam in disbelief… Raoul was on the touchline, back in Spain! Raoul could not see Adam as he looked up, just the clear blue sky of the Barcelona day but he was ecstatically happy to be back and waved hoping that Adam could see. He could, and he couldn't believe his eyes as he watched Raoul run down the tunnel to continue with his life.

Adam stayed at the pub to watch the match but, to his disappointment, he didn't see Raoul on screen again. But as he was about to leave, Adam's phone beeped the receipt of a text message:

"I think we were touched by God my friend. Thank you for your help and please accept a gift in gratitude for your help. Please look at your account. And

do not ask me how I got the details! My only request is that I would ask that the incident is never talked about. Thank you. Raoul".

Adam quickly checked his on-line account on his phone and his jaw physically dropped . . . one million euros had been deposited into Adam's almost empty account! He tried to compose himself and left the pub as calmly as he could.

He tried to reply to the text later but no replies were accepted, as if Raoul wanted to draw a line under the event.

There were days when Adam was sorely tempted to break Raoul's confidence but Raoul but he knew if the story got out there would be a media frenzy, an irreversible taint to Raoul's reputation. So Adam never told a soul—who would believe him anyway? He couldn't resist trying the "lifting the player from the pitch" trick again, several times in fact, but it never worked.

The money did make a difference. After helping his brother and his parents, he decided to change direction and concentrate more on his music. He still played in the same band though, albeit with some new equipment. They were good friends. And they still played at the Plough and Harrow.

Three months later, quite by chance, Barcelona were playing there when the band were in the pub. Inevitably, Adam looked out for Raoul . . . and there he was! Still at the top of his game, still full-sized and still in Barcelona.

"And there's Raoul waving to someone in the crowd" said the commentator as the camera moved in. But Adam knew he was waving at him, straight towards the cameras! Raoul gestured a big "thumbs up" and smiled.

"Probably waving at his agent" the commentator continued, "for negotiating that out of season transfer deal . . . I'm sure the agent did very well out of that!"

Adam smiled and turned round to his new drum kit.

"My round I think, what are you drinking?"

The Force

It was Clive's 60th birthday and what do you get the man who has everything? Cars, gadgets, holidays... Clive had them all. But Matt thought he'd found a certain something that his father-in-law wouldn't forget.

The party was going well and Matt was waiting for the time to spring the surprise on Clive, and now was the time. He walked up to the stage and borrowed the microphone from the disco DJ.

"Ladies and gentlemen" announced Matt, trying to moderate his volume on the mic. "As you know we're here to celebrate Clive's 60th birthday". A big cheer rose up. "Come up here then you old codger!" Clive got out of his chair and sheepishly approached the stage to a wave of applause. With a hand on Clive's shoulder Matt continued.

"I just want to say that, Clive, you mean a lot to us all and I'd like to thank you for being like a Dad to me" A lump appeared in his throat "Thank you for everything you've done for me and Claire." The two men hugged. They had grown very close and Clive couldn't wish for a better partner for his daughter.

"Anyway, enough of the emotional stuff" said Matt *"Happy birthday to you, happy birthday to you.."* Matt lead the chorus to the end ... *"Happy Birthday tooo youuu".* A cheer rose up.

"Now we were thinking Clive, what *do* you get the man who has got everything? And then it came to us"

Matt signalled the DJ and the Star Wars theme music burst out of the speakers. The audience were suspended in a state of smiling confusion.

Matt nodded to the dark-suited manager waiting in the lobby to his left, and then out the little fellow walked ... a dwarf dressed as Yoda, complete with rubber mask, robes and a green light sabre, strolled out towards Clive waving at the audience, laughter spreading across the room like a Mexican wave!

Clive looked at Matt and smiled. He had been caught good and proper! Matt knew he loved Star Wars and when he saw he could hire a dwarf Yoda for the evening, he knew his search for the perfect gift was over. His manager had even driven him all the way down from Bristol for the occasion! Yoda waved his light sabre and shook Clive's hand. Then, without saying a word, he slipped a pair of handcuffs on them both! Clive was to be handcuffed to a dwarf Yoda for the evening! Matt loved it, and his huge amusement had overcome the feeling of it being slightly wrong.

"Thanks Matt!" said Clive sarcastically, still in shock, but smiling.

"We've got him for three hours so have fun! He wasn't cheap!" laughed Matt.

Of course, Yoda was the focus of attention in the room, waving at everyone, not saying a word.

"The force is with you, it is!" joked Clive's brother.

"Ha! Very good!" Clive was in truth a little uncomfortable that a dwarf had hired himself out. It *was* funny and definitely memorable but it was bordering on people laughing *at* him, not *with* him. "Not a million miles away from having a token black man or ginger person handcuffed to you for a laugh" he thought, not wanting to say it within ear-shot of the dwarf.

Clive sat down and the dwarf sat next to him, his legs dangling from the cushioned velvet social club bench seat, bobbing up and down to the music, much to the amusement of all around him.

"Are you OK in there?" asked Clive, trying to make small-talk.

The dwarf didn't respond, just bobbed to the music and waved to anyone nearby.

"Your round I think Clive" said his brother.

"Could *you?*" asked Clive holding up his handcuffed wrist.

"Well, I *would* but my leg is playing up a little" his brother joked, holding the back of his knee.

"Oh *really!*" smiled Clive. Clive got up and the dwarf hopped off the seat to follow him to the bar. From the barman's vantage point, all you could see was Clive, so he leaned over the counter to check he was still there. "Hello my friend!" The dwarf waved.

"Has he got a name?"

"Hasn't said a word yet!" said Clive under his breath.

"*Yoda* it is then! Does the Jedi knight want a drink?"

"Would you like a drink?" asked Clive miming bringing a glass to his lips.

Yoda looked across to his manager, dark and suited standing in the lobby. The manager shook his head. Yoda shook his head, refusing the drink.

"Who is that in the shadows, the Dark Lord?!"

Clive laughed. "Are you sure?" he mouthed to the dwarf under the music. The dwarf nodded.

Clive picked up his beer and returned to the table, supping some beer. It was shaping into a great night and the room had started to buzz.

"You're not sitting there for long!" said his brother "Let's have a boogie!"

Clive and his small companion danced through the club, weaving through the crowd, everyone smiling as they approached, taking the opportunity to have a little dance with the dwarf. Yoda was very obliging, waving, dancing, swaying his light sabre . . . the "YMCA", "Oops up side your head", the "Macarena" . . . this was a dwarf with all the moves. All the time the dark manager hovered in the lobby, arms crossed, overseeing. Caught up in the dancing, Matt remembered he needed to pay the man, so he walked over to the lobby.

"It's all there and a bit extra, he is *fantastic*!" shouted Matt over the pumping music, the six pints of cider taking effect. The manager smiled and nodded, tucking the envelope into his inside jacket pocket, all the time never taking his eyes off Yoda.

"How's things in the dwarf hire business then?" asked Matt. "Good" said the manager without changing his expression, eyes still fixed on Yoda.

"Good, good" said Matt awkwardly "Help yourself to drinks from the bar".

"I will" replied the dark suited manager.

"Bloody hell" said Matt joining Clive on the dance floor, "his manager bloody *is* Darth Vadar! I expected him to breathe funny!"

"And you expected a dwarf hiring manager to be your average man-in-the-street?!"

"Ha! Perhaps not!" Matt agreed.

"I need a pee! What am I going to do?!" said Clive concerned.

"Well, I think you'll just have to use one hand!"

Clive walked up to the manager in the lobby "I need to go to the loo" he shouted "Can you un-cuff me for five minutes?"

Expressionless, the manager nodded. "Thank God" thought Clive.

"Hot in there it is!" joked a work colleague standing next to Clive at the urinals, sweat trickling down his forehead. "Have you lost him then?"

"Only to come in here I think!" replied Clive.

"It's genius!" his colleague beamed. Clive wasn't quite so convinced.

As he left the toilet, Clive noticed the manager slipping Yoda something to eat under his thick rubber mask, almost like giving a dog a treat.

"Must be warm in there!" Clive mentioned as the handcuffs were clicked back on. "Both of you please help yourself to drinks from the bar".

"Come on Birthday Boy!" said Clive's brother grabbing his free arm and dragging him back to the dancefloor. The music was pumping, the room jumping, and sweat dripping . . . Clive was starting to flag now, he was 60 after all. After another half an hour Clive could sense the dwarf was slowing too.

"We're going to sit down for a while and cool off!" he shouted. The dwarf nodded, just managing one wave of his light sabre as they sat down.

"What a night Clive!" said his brother, "Matt played a blinder didn't he?!"

"Yes, I'll not forget this in a hurry!" Clive agreed.

As Clive chatted to his guests, he was conscious that the dwarf was just sitting there, almost being ignored now, and Clive was starting to feel uncomfortable. Yes it *had* been funny but it was a *person* he'd had cuffed to his arm all evening, not some plaything.

"Are you OK in there?" he said "Let me get you a drink. You've definitely earned it!"

There was no response . . . motionless. "Hello!" Clive said loudly, shaking the dwarf gently on the shoulder. There was still no response and Yoda slumped sideways onto the cushioned bench seat. Concerned, Clive pulled the thick rubber mask off . . . It was just a child . . . a young girl with long brown hair, no more than eight, red-faced, not breathing . . .

Panicking, Clive cradled her in his arms and stood up. *"Help!"* he screamed, looking across to the lobby over the still-heaving dancefloor . . . but the manager was nowhere to be seen.

Fast Food

"It's happened again Marjorie!"

This really was too much for Tarquin. It was an expensive microwave and this was the second time this month. Last week it was a cup of tea, this time a large lasagne! He looked at the open microwave door. He *knew* he'd put it in there...15 mins it said on the box. It pinged, he opened the door, but now it was gone!

"That's it I'm phoning the shop tomorrow, they can have it back!"

In Kev and Sharon's flat in Romford, the microwave pinged.

"Did you put the tea on?" asked Kev, shouting to be heard over the TV.

"No! I was waiting for you to do it!"

Kev looked at the large steaming lasagne behind the door of the microwave and smiled.

"It's happened again Sharon!"

The Tiger Treat Restaurant

Thirty degrees was hot enough, but with the humidity of an October in Rajasthan, it felt like Tom was stepping into a greenhouse as he left the air-conditioned coach. Luckily it was only a short walk from the car park to the cool of the "Tiger Treat Restaurant", a welcome break after the three hour coach journey.

"No wonder they're extinct!" joked Tom to a fellow passenger as he pointed up to the bright red "Tiger Treat Restaurant" lettering on the high white sign with a red border. The red and white theme extended to the whole of the single-storey building, bright and crisp against the cloudless blue sky.

"Phew, thank God for air-con!" said Tom to no-one in particular as he entered the combination of restaurant and huge gift shop. There was very little time when Tom wasn't talking and this was no exception. It was pleasantly cool in the shop but the prices were high and the staff persistent.

"This is the god Ganesh. Brings good luck. Very reasonable! 1500 rupees" pressed one of the many Indian assistants.

"Do you *actually* serve Tiger in here?" joked Tom, ignoring the sales pitch.

"I beg your pardon sir?"

"Tiger Treat Restaurant? I didn't think you were allowed to eat them! What is it? Tiger burgers?!"

It was the third time that morning someone had tried to make that joke, but the assistant smiled politely and backed away, recognising a difficult sale when he saw one.

It had got to the point on the coach where others were now tolerating Tom. He always had something to say and frequently said it. He considered himself the life and soul of the party and, in small doses he came across amiably enough but most had had their fill by now. More sympathetic passengers had suggested that maybe there was a back story "Wasn't allowed to speak as a child . . . "

"Locked in a basement for a few years perhaps . . . ". But in truth his childhood was as happy and balanced as anyone's.

"No wonder, they're extinct!" Tom grinned to the third victim who had foolishly smiled in his direction.

"Pardon?"

"Tiger Treat Restaurant? I think it's tiger burgers they're serving!"

"Ahh, yes" winced the victim "Let's hope not!" he said backing away. During the trip, quite a few people had started to back away, not that Tom had noticed. He was too busy thinking about what he was going to say next.

"I'm sure he means well" some had said, but in truth he really didn't. Spectacularly self-centred, his Facebook page was a barrage of trivia broadcasted to his 4500 "friends", who really weren't concerned about what he had just eaten.

After a while, the Indian shop manager had noticed a gradual migration of people away from the gift shop and into the cheaper "snacks" area, and even outside! Tom was driving customers away and something had to be done!

Co-incidentally, it was today that someone needed to be chosen. The arrangement was one from every five groups and it was normally a joint decision between the manager and the tour guide, but this time the person had almost chosen themselves.

"Hello sir" smiled the polite Indian restaurant owner.

"Oh hello" said Tom "You don't actually *serve* Tiger here do you?!"

"Ah, no sir, we do not" smiled the owner "but if you like, I can show you why the establishment got that name?"

"That would be very nice. Thank you" smiled Tom. The owner led Tom through the small restaurant area and out into a poorly lit lobby. He switched on the lights.

"I think you will like this sir. It is not everyone who gets to experience this"

"I'm very flattered. Thank you" replied Tom excited.

The owner held back the door to a large hall and ushered Tom in. The hall was dimly lit with large branches leaning against the walls and earth and hay on the floor.

"That's a funny smell" said Tom. He didn't see the first tiger as it leapt on his back and knocked him to the floor ... and he only saw the second tiger's face fleetingly as it pressed into his neck, its huge teeth closing on his throat. For the briefest moment Tom smelt its musky fur and felt its warm breath before the beast tore out his throat, removing so much that death was instantaneous.

It had been some time since the tigers' last meal and Tom being on the portly side, was indeed a special treat for them.

As the tigers feasted, a roar could be heard faintly in the gift shop.

"What was that?" asked a customer at the till.

"Sounds like thunder again" replied the young cashier, "but you might be lucky"

"I hope it doesn't rain" said the customer "we're on a tiger safari this afternoon"

"Ahh, such beautiful beasts!" said the cashier.

"Would you like a small tiger?" he said pointing to the many tiger related gifts on the counter.

"Only 700 rupees."

Tears of a Clown

"Is that the best you can do?!" snapped a jaded Detective Sergeant.
"There's no need to be rude about it!" sniffed Mrs Jackson, upset after going over the details of the theft of her handbag again. "I'm telling you *exactly* what I saw!"

"Yes, I'm sure you are Mrs Jackson" said the detective, handing her his handkerchief, "and we'd like to help but you need to give us a little more to go on. OK, let's go over your statement again"

"Reddish hair you said?"

"Yes, *bright* red really" sniffed Mrs Jackson.

"Any idea of age?"

"Hard to tell"

"But you're sure about the large shoes?"

"Oh yes"

"And the red and yellow diamond matching jacket and trousers?"

"Yes" she sniffed.

"And, just so we are clear on this Mrs Jackson, he *definitely* had a white face and a bright red nose?"

"Oh yes, I'm absolutely certain about that" said Mrs Jackson, perking up.

"Any distinctive sounds, Mrs Jackson? His voice?"

"Yes it was quite high pitched and he was laughing"

"Mmm" said the detective "*laughing* you say..." not bothering to write it down.

"And the handbag, did it look like that one?" said the detective pointing to Mrs Jackson's unremarkable back-up handbag with his pen.

"Yes, very similar actually"

"Mmm" sighed the policeman.

"Well, we'll try of course, it's got a case number" said the detective trying to sound hopeful. "We'll try to get it back for you Mrs Jackson but if I'm being honest, I wouldn't hold your breath".

"Thank you" said a calmer Mrs Jackson handing back his damp handkerchief.

"That's OK" smiled the detective, "you keep it".

Mrs Jackson left the interview room and walked up the corridor towards the reception desk.

"Do you mind if I use the toilet?" she asked one of the uniformed officers.

"No, please go ahead" he gestured.

Mrs Jackson adjusted her nose in the mirror and checked her face paint before leaving the building, out into the hustle and bustle of the capital. Being lunchtime, the pavements were full of clowns shopping, eating and going about their business before returning to their jobs for the afternoon.

Tentatively, Mrs Jackson stepped into the colourful throng, swept along with the tide of clowns moving almost as one down the wide pavement.

She didn't like it being so busy, more accustomed to life in the suburbs.

"What if someone dropped their nose?" she thought "They'd be trampled!"

It wasn't far to the station and Mrs Jackson kept shuffling along, all the time keeping a tight grip on her handbag.

Same as it Ever Was

In the high village, a large black water buffalo stood silently, loosely tethered to a tree in the dry dirt yard.

"Watch your legs, Jen!" said Edna to her fellow passenger, who's feet were dangling from the edge of the camel-drawn cart, worryingly close to the wheel.

It was a sedate ride up the dirt track through the lower village up to the old higher village that they were visiting as part of their Indian holiday. Four camel-drawn carts, six people to a cart, each camel with a turbaned handler leading them through the idyllic scene. Legs swaying off the flat bed carts, women in Saris waving from the field, children chasing after the carts, some jumping on for the ride, the low sun silhouetting the palm trees and ancient fort on the ridge of the hill. Occasionally the camels would be passed by four people on a moped but they didn't seem to be phased, their huge feet plodding along pulling steadily uphill, looking slightly uncomfortable in the occasional downhill parts as the weight of the cart helped pushed them along.

Edna sat with her legs swinging from the back of the cart and the following camel was catching up, its large head looming straight in front of her. "Woah! That's close enough!"

A small boy hitching a ride on the steps at the back of the cart was smiling permanently and held his hand out for some money.

"Sorry I don't have any" said Edna "Would you like a pen?" Edna had bought ten cheap jewelled pens the day before for just such an occasion. The boy was very pleased, jumping off the cart, now the envy of his friends.

As the camels ambled on, a group of older teenage boys passed on a donkey-drawn cart coming the other way. "Hello! Hello!" they shouted in a forced English accent. "Hello! No thank you" they said "Hello, no thank you!"

Edna suspected they were involved in selling the many trinkets that were being offered at the more popular sites during the trip and they had heard the words "no, thank you" in English quite a lot!

All in all, it was turning out to be a perfect birthday for Edna. She had always wanted to come to India and despite the hustle and poverty, it was everything she had hoped it would be and more. She had her concerns to start with, travelling on her own, but people couldn't have been more friendly. The last couple of days she had particularly loved as they had been off the beaten track, a chance to see a bit of the real India.

As the cart pulled into the village, it didn't disappoint. Young bare-footed children smiling and running towards the carts, a large dirt yard dotted with trees, shacks surrounding the yard with large black water buffalos standing silently, loosely tethered to the trees. Goats tended their young kids that bleated and stumbled over the uneven ground, some perched unsteadily on the occasional rocks. Mostly it was women in the village, beautifully dressed in bright blue, yellow and purple saris, colour everywhere. Edna could not stop smiling. It struck her that the scene was almost biblical, unchanged for thousands of years. A simple life, but a lot of smiling and happiness.

A lady in a purple sari approached Edna smiling and offered a baby goat for her to hold.

"Oh yes please!" she beamed cradling the little goat in her arms, traces of the umbilical cord still present. This was the start of most of the women in the group wanting to hold a baby goat, with many photographs taken by their other halves.

The main purpose of their visit was a cookery demonstration from the villagers and eventually the party gathered around the front of one of the larger shacks to watch an older lady prepare chapattis and a curry dish. Blue and red sari draped in the dust, crouching bare foot on her haunches, she effortlessly shaped the chapattis, cooking them over a fire pit on a thick metal plate. To a rapt audience, she then prepared the curry ingredients, throwing in pinches of this spice and that, smoke spiralling up from the pit on the hot, still day, the sun starting to disappear behind the shack, the sky a calm golden amber.

The smell filled the dusty quiet yard as the visitors looked on intently while the children of the village sat quietly along the edge of the shack on the steps, more interested in the visitors than the cooking. One older teenage girl particularly caught Edna's eye. She sat on the steps leaning back against the wall of the shack, her arms resting on her knees, looking over the group and never smiling. Her dress was less traditional, more Western and her eyes were the brightest blue, eyes that could look through to your very soul, "eyes that could turn you to stone" Edna thought. During the whole demonstration the girl didn't move, just sat there with her arms on her knees studying people who had gathered to watch her aunt cooking, as if overseeing the whole affair.

Eventually, a gentleman of the village offered the visitors a sample of the food. Most people accepted, including Edna.

"Delicious!" she nodded towards the cook.

Only one or two refused, "I've avoided Delhi-Belly so far and I'm not going to tempt fate with this! Smells good though"

The light was fading and it was time to return to the lower village. After a round of applause for the demonstration, Edna and her travelling companions returned to the camels and carts. She was pleased to get the same place at the back of the cart and looked forward to seeing the whole scene unfold for her again at sunset. As the carts were waved out of the village, Edna noticed that the baby goats were being gathered up and put in to a small pen by the shack in the cooking area. "Must be time for bed for them" she thought.

As the dust from the carts drifted down the track, the teenage girl stood up and called over to the waving girls at the entrance.

"Have they gone yet?"

"Yes. All clear!"

The blue-eyed girl smiled, flipped the lid open on a small wooden box on a post and pressed the button. There was a short burst of an alarm and everyone got up off the steps and into the yard, in a well-rehearsed drill.

"What was that?" said Edna as the alarm echoed off the hills.

"Probably monkeys" replied a fellow traveller who was prone to guessing the answers to such questions.

When the teenage girl was sure everyone was clear, she pressed the button again and the wooden sides of the shacks started to lower slowly into the ground, slowly revealing smart contemporary blue-glazed fronted buildings, eventually the wooden frontings disappearing completely. The new buildings were equipped with modern furniture, flat screen entertainment centres and all the expected Wi-Fi connected trappings of modern life.

The blue eyed-girl saw her aunt starting to gather the cooking plates and utensils. "Just throw them in the dishwasher!" she called to her.

"No, I am fine" her aunt smiled, preferring to use the water from the well.

The children were not running around anymore, all engrossed with their phones, including the teenager, who could see from a text that their first visit tomorrow was 10.45am.

All was quiet now … the goats in their pens, the children preoccupied and the black water buffalo standing silently, loosely tethered to a tree.

Cappuccino

"Cappuccino please" said Kristian as his breath steamed on the frosty railway platform.

"Sorry we only serve coffee sir" replied the small Malaysian barista.

"Yes, so I'll have a cappuccino please?" replied Kristian confused.

"No, I'm sorry sir, you can't have a *cup of tea now*, we only serve coffee!"

Kristian had experienced some difficulties with people understanding his Birmingham accent before.

"No, I'd like a capp-u-cci-no please!" he smiled.

"I'm sorry sir, but you can't have a cup of tea *now* or at any other time as we do not serve it! There is another shop inside the station that do a range of teas"

Kristian was dumb-founded and turned to the lady behind him in the queue.

"Is it me?"

"There *is* a shop in the station that does tea" said the lady, keen to get served.

"But I want a cappuccino!"

"Well, the quickest way would be to go to the other shop I think. It's very nice"

"What!" said Kristian incredulously. The queue was getting anxious.

"Tell you what" he said turning back to the barista "I'll just have a coffee!"

"I'm sorry sir they're mine"

"What, you don't sell coffee now!"

"Well no, not really sir, they're mine" he said pointing towards the bag of toffees on the counter.

"No!" laughed Kristian "*Coffeeee*, I'd like a coffeeee!"

"Look, have one of mine if you like sir" said the barista offering his bag, eager to keep the queue moving.

"I can't, I'm diabetic!" said Kristian.

"Well why do you ask for sweets sir?" said the barista.

"You shouldn't really" interrupted the lady behind him in the queue "My husband nearly lost his foot to diabetes"

"OK, what's going on here?! Is there some sort of hidden camera?" asked Kristian starting to lose his patience "All I want is a bloody coffee on a cold morning! Is that too much to ask?!"

"And I have already offered you one of mine sir!"

"Can you hurry up please!" shouted the lady "we've all got trains to catch!"

"Do you mind Madam!" replied the annoyed barista, "I am working as hard as I can and there is no need to be rude!" He turned away muttering under his breath as he wiped down the spout of the coffee machine "Middle-class commuters . . . think they own the place"

"Hey I heard that!" shouted Kristian, fitting that description himself. "There's no need to mock her!"

"Mocha?" smiled the barista "Certainly sir, why didn't you say?!"

The Circle of the Grand Counsel

"Goodbye" smiled Manjit holding open the heavy door for the young lady with crutches, "Have a good week".

"Yes, you too" she replied as she carefully picked her way down the stairs in the old British Legion building where Manjit's counselling room was based.

It was a scene that Tony saw every week, the young lady's regular appointment being just before his each Friday.

"Hello Tony! How are you?" Manjit said smiling.

"Not bad, thank you"

"Not bad?!" he replied, "then what are you doing *here*?!" he joked. Manjit had a good rapport with most of his clients, but always respectful, always professional. And it was true that things were not that bad for Tony. He had only had three sessions but they were helping him lay the ghosts of a messy divorce to rest, so they didn't creep into his daily life too often.

"Do you mind if I open the window?" said Manjit standing on a chair and struggling to slide up the old sticky sash window.

"No that's fine"

"I won't leave it open for long, it's just the lady before had a stinker of a cold and that's the last thing I want just before Christmas"

"Dead right" agreed Tony. Manjit's down-to-earth friendly approach put his clients at ease, as if they were chatting to a friend. He would draw on his own experiences to help: the loss of his father, relationship difficulties, religious dilemmas, other client's experiences … they helped the lady with the crutches deal with her accident, Tony with his divorce and Colin at 10.00 deal with the sudden loss of his parents. He was the master of the analogy too, once saying to Tony "It's like letting a troublesome genie out of a bottle. If it's in there too long, it's desperate to get out and, when it does for the first time, it goes a bit crazy. But after a while, it's happy to go back in again and it's not bursting to get out anymore. You and the genie are living more in harmony"

It was Friday and, as much as he loved his job, Manjit felt a little drained.

"I think it's time" he thought and looked up Tobias's number on his phone.

For Manjit, it worked out about every other month, things getting to a point where he had taken on board enough and he needed to see a counsellor *himself* to download some of the burden he had helped to shoulder.

"Where has that couple of months gone?" joked Tobias as he opened the door of his rooms to Manjit.

"Soon be Christmas" smiled Manjit, pleased to be in Tobias's easy company.

The counselling room was traditionally decorated on the first floor of an old Georgian house that smelt like an old church. There were two single comfortable leather chairs facing each other, a very similar arrangement to Manjit's room, except this was a little bigger and a little more recently decorated. Tobias was older, 55 to Manjit's 36 and Manjit considered him wiser.

"So what would you like to talk about today?" asked Tobias through his short beard.

"Where do I start!" replied Manjit

"Anywhere you like!" smiled Tobias "How about a cup of tea or coffee?"

"Tea would be great"

"Thought so, I've made one here" he said passing it to Manjit.

"Thank you. You know, there is one case I *would* like to run past you..."

And Manjit went on to describe Mrs Jackson..."overnight with no warning or signs, her husband announced that he wasn't physically attracted to her anymore"

"Oh... any history of bisexuality?"

"Apparently not, just woke up one morning and told her he *loved* her but he didn't want her sexually anymore. The poor woman was distraught"

Once the door was open, Manjit went on to discuss a number of cases, particularly an attempted suicide of a man in his early twenties that had perhaps had more of an effect on him than he'd realised. Tobias listened and reflected and counselled and at the end of the session Manjit felt better and walked a little lighter, as he always did. As he had been seeing Tobias for about a year now, he felt comfortable enough to ask the next question.

"Do you have many counsellors and psychotherapists as clients?"

"Yes, probably eleven or twelve now"

"So who do *you* go to for sessions like this? You know, to offload."

Tobias smiled "I've been seeing a gentleman called Benjy for years. He's not local but he's very good. And his beard is longer"

"What?" questioned the clean-shaven Manjit.

"Seems to be a basic rule" smiled Tobias with a twinkle in his eye, "the longer the beard the wiser the man!"

"I'd better hurry up and grow one then" laughed Manjit, "I must be losing customers left, right and centre!"

"What about Benjy then? Who does *he* see?" enquired Manjit.

"Ahh well, would you believe he supposedly sees the Grand Counsel himself"

"Who?"

"The Grand Counsel. Apparently he only has fifty counsellors on his books at any time and recently Benjy has been allowed to see him. A great privilege!"

"You make him sound like some sort of king!" said Manjit.

"Well there's no crown, but apparently there is a throne!"

"You're joking!"

"Apparently not" replied Tobias "and many steps up to it!"

"Ah, don't tell me" joked Manjit "the throne is made of swords with fires lining its approach, with knights and swords ..."

"Ha, ha! No not quite, he's a jolly chap supposedly"

"What, more like Father Christmas?" joked Manjit.

"Well, yes, from what I have heard! Although you realise that Father Christmas doesn't exist"

"Oh, break it to me gently why don't you!" replied Manjit with false dismay.

"I can help you with this ..." replied Tobias earnestly "Now, how does that make you *feel?*" They both roared with laughter.

Dabbing his eyes with his hankerchief, Manjit asked "Seriously, like Father Christmas?"

"Well no red suit and reindeer but an impressive beard and very jolly apparently"

"Do you have to sit on his knee?" smiled Manjit.

"I hope not!"

"Does he allow visitors?" asked Manjit.

"Apparently not. It's all a bit mysterious and I can't get Benjy to talk about it much"

"A vow of silence!" Manjit announced dramatically.

"Not quite! I suppose he just wants to get on with things undisturbed"

"But I've never heard of him in any of the journals, never even heard of him at all 'til now ... how come?"

"He's a private man and doesn't court the fame or the money" said Tobias.

"Mmm ... so he counsel's for free does he" said Manjit doubtfully.

"I have no idea. Sorry Manjit, I'm afraid that's our time used up"

Over the coming weeks Manjit thought a lot about the "Grand Counsel".

"Who the hell is he?" He felt certain he would find references on the web, Facebook, Twitter, the usual haunts that normally describe exactly where people are and what they are eating ... nothing ... "you'd think there would be something, a comment on a forum somewhere" Manjit thought, but no.

Two months went by and it was time for Manjit to visit Tobias again.

He settled down into the leather chair and smiled as Tobias passed him a cup of tea. "I know this sounds strange but I'm going to hi-jack this meeting to talk about the Grand Counsel as I've thought of little else since we last met!"

"Certainly" replied Tobias "I'm here to talk about whatever you want, but I'm not sure how much I can help"

"Have you ever been tempted to find out more about him?" asked Manjit.

"Well yes, he's an intriguing character isn't he" agreed Tobias "but I've been so busy lately, I'm just keeping my head above water"

"I can help you with that!" joked Manjit. Tobias grinned and chuckled.

"All I know is that he apparently sees him at 11am on the first of every month"

"I know this sounds odd, and bordering on unprofessional, but have you ever been tempted to follow Benjy to a session" asked Manjit.

"Of course not!" Tobias protested.

"No, you wouldn't I'm sure". He was fairly sure that Tobias wouldn't, but Manjit decided at that moment that *he* would.

The session progressed well. "Good to see you Tobias and we'll speak soon"

"Indeed we will. Take care" replied Tobias.

Benjy was a lot easier for Manjit to find on the web than the Grand Counsel. Soon he had photos, an address, what he eaten for breakfast, too much information if anything. And in two days time, it would be the first of March.

He felt uneasy but he would be very discreet and keep his distance, despite an overwhelming urge to just ring Benjy's doorbell and quiz him about it.

"Who was this bearded man on the throne?" Part of him suspected Tobias of fabricating the whole thing.

At 10.00am on the first of March, Manjit sat on the bench opposite Benjy's smart ground floor flat. The traffic was light, the birds were singing and there was starting to be some warmth in the sun that hit his face and his overcoat.

It took a while but eventually Benjy's door opened and he emerged, turning left up the street. Hoping he would be walking to his meeting, Manjit started to follow Benjy at a discreet distance . . . he had seen the films.

It was quite a walk, down the arrow straight street until Benjy turned sharp right into the underground station.

"Ah, he's getting a train, Bit further than I thought…" Keeping his distance, Manjit followed Benjy down the steps. The underground hall was quiet, only a few people dotted about in the large space left after the morning rush. Benjy walked briskly towards the corner of the hall, away from the escalators, away from anything in fact, and in the corner there was a small white painted door marked "Private". It was a door that thousands of people could walk past every day and wouldn't notice. Looking over his shoulder, Benjy unlocked the door.

"Damn!" thought Manjit "He's going to lock it behind him!". After a moment, he approached the door and tried to turn its old brass knob … and to Manjit's delight the door opened. He walked through the door as quietly as he could into the dimly lit tiled underground pedestrian tunnel, one that was obviously no longer used and had escaped renovation for many years. He couldn't see Benjy but he carried on through the gently curving tunnel, a never-ending corner that you couldn't see round, gradually descending, each step amplified by the hard tiled walls. Until he came across a portcullis-like gate that prevented any further access.

"Damn!" he cursed, looking for any latch or key but there was none. It looked like the end of the road but to his surprise, the gate slowly rose, the tunnel filling with a cacophony of scraping metal and chains. Cautiously, he walked through and carried on. The tunnel continued to curve but he just kept on walking,.. "I've come this far", until the scraping of metal again bouncing through the tunnel stopped him. It was the gate lowering behind him but there was nothing he could do, he was too far down the tunnel to stop it now.

"This is ridiculous" Manjit thought, now seriously doubting the wisdom of following Benjy at all. Eventually the downward slope of tunnel gradually levelled out and opened up into a space that made Manjit stop walking and stare, mouth open, trying to take in what was before him.

"Oh my God". The space was majestic, emerald green stone with huge vertical pillars disappearing into a ceiling as high as any cathedral he'd seen. Fires burned in large standards along all the walkways and the walls flickered and danced. Manjit walked in, his steps echoing … but there was no sign of Benjy at all. In front of him across the great hall was a set of stone steps and at the top, he could see a throne.

"Oh my God!" he repeated, "Tobias was right!"

Manjit hadn't heard anything but he jumped as he noticed two knights fully dressed in bronze armour appear at his sides.

"Don't be alarmed" one knight said. But Manjit was alarmed, unaccustomed to being approached by knights.

"Please approach the throne" said the knight to his left, gently taking his arm.

"What is this?!" said Manjit.

"Come with us and you have nothing to fear". He didn't feel threatened, so he allowed the knights to lead him to the foot of the stone steps, one holding either arm.

He could see the throne better now. It was huge with an ornate gold frame, upholstered in a rich red velvet with a crest on the back. The knights escorted him half-way up the steps where they left him and proceeded to stand either side of the throne, facing him. In the flickering firelight Manjit could see some movement and something emerged from the background . . . it was him! The Grand Counsel! Just like Tobias had described him, except he walked out quite deftly on his crutches, before leaning them on the side of his throne and turning to sit down, his huge blonde beard laying over a green and gold velvet gown. Then he took off his beard and smiled.

Manjit couldn't believe it . . . it was the lady who he had been helping for weeks with her accident.

"We have had our eye on you, Manjit" the lady smiled "and I have been very impressed with the service you have given me. In short, we think you are ready" The knights at her side slowly removed their bronze helmets and Tobias and Benjy both smiled down on Manjit.

"Welcome to the Circle of the Grand Counsel!" said Tobias.

In the Cool of the Evening

To Maria, it always seemed to be a sunny day at the graveyard.

"Of course it is!" she realised, "How many people would choose to visit during a storm?!" Maybe the odd person who enjoyed the drama, but not many.

She liked to sit on the bench at the top of the hill that overlooked the "Lawns Cemetery". It was aptly named with newly mown lawns separating the lines of well-kept graves, rows of white and black marble standing to attention, reflecting the low sun. Maria knew those lawns would be gradually used up in time but she hoped that wouldn't change the peaceful atmosphere of quiet contemplation. She had lost her mother the previous year and had been through the various stages of grief but was now at a point where she could sit and remember without immediately crying, even smiling occasionally as she recalled her mother's eccentricities ... the way she once asked a waiter if the prawns were "Atlantic Prawns" faking a knowledge of prawns that she never had; the way she used to swim out far to sea on her own when Maria was a child, until she worried if her mother would return; the way she boiled vegetables until all colour had disappeared and the water was green ...

She had already been over to her mother's grave to say "hello" and to tidy up any leaves or old flowers. It always seemed to be muddy down there, even on a bright day, a consequence of the soil being regularly disturbed she thought. But now Maria sat on the seat at the top of the hill, a peaceful place where thoughts could run through her head at their own pace, the last of the sun on her face on this crisp late January day. She smiled as she watched someone clearing up Christmas decorations from a grave, a holly wreath and some gold tinsel. Everyone else seemed to be in a rush to get decorations down by before 12th night to avoid the bad luck but there was no such rush here, some graves even having whole decorated miniature trees left up ... "can't be too worried about the luck here" she thought. On the seat her thoughts tended to wander aimlessly.

"I wonder if there are more worms in *this* field than there are next door?" she thought rather morbidly. "What a thought!" she laughed to herself, thinking it was probably time to leave, especially as a chill wind had started to blow and clouds were gathering, a few large drops falling on the tarmac path, with the promise of more to come. Maria got up and walked to the car and, as she knocked the mud off her wellingtons and slipped into her driving shoes, the heavens opened. Quickly shutting the boot, she jumped into the driving seat just as rain started to cascade down the windscreen. As she approached the exit of the graveyard, she instinctively felt in her coat pocket for her mobile phone ... it wasn't there ... so she stopped and had a proper look ... no, no sign of it.

"Damn it" she thought "probably slipped out at the bench".

She drove back and sure enough there it was. The sharp shower was starting to ease and, as she picked up her phone, she heard a rustle to her left ...

"Odd, must be the wind" she thought.

Maria jumped back in her car, aware that she seemed to be the last to leave that day, closing time fast approaching.

Driving through the cemetery gates, she waved to the very smartly dressed old man waiting to lock up for the day. "Old-school suit wearer" she thought "or maybe going to an interview".

Jack locked the gates and started to walk back up the gentle hill to the graveyard, where people had started to come out for the evening. They reached up through the earth and climbed out, many using their gravestone to help. They mingled smiling and greeting each other, resplendent in their Sunday-best suits and fine dresses, all without a trace of mud. Every night it was the same quite grand occasion, not unlike a ball on the Titanic.

"I thought they'd never leave today" said Bernadette. "They can really drag the atmosphere down here sometimes, don't you think?"

"Yes and look what they leave!" smiled Maggie, holding up faded dead flowers "Kids, eh! Who'd have them!"

"I've got some beautiful ones here though" said Maude proudly.

"Here, you have some Fred". Fred died in 1897. He was fine but he didn't get flowers any more.

"Thank you Maude!" smiled Fred "Is Jack back from the gates yet?"

"Here he comes now" Jack was walking up the path with a spring in his step that belied his 174 years.

"Well let's get this party started!" smiled Bernadette clapping her hands together, as she was joined by her friends from all over The Lawns.

Shaved Santa

Bob didn't want to be Father Christmas. It's not that he didn't like children, he had two older ones of his own, but John from number 87 would have done a much better job … he had the figure and the jolly demeanour, only trouble was he hadn't turned up and there were twenty-five kids expecting to see the man in red. The village carol service was always the same, some carols, some mulled wine, the odd turn from the children *and* a visit from Father Christmas for the youngsters. A present of some sweets and a glimpse of the man himself a few days before the big day, proof that he was on his rounds, so be good for goodness sake.

"Quick, get into the kitchen and I'll bring you the gear!" said Martin the compere, trying to rescue the situation.

"No problem" Bob lied, and sneaked out to the small village hall kitchen.

"Well done sir!" said Tommy who was helping with the mulled wine "The gear is in the carrier bag down there"

"Great" replied Bob reluctantly, not relishing wearing the unwashed Santa beard that had festered in the bag over the years. He hurriedly pulled on the stretchy red robe edged with white fur and put on the hat but he couldn't find the beard.

"Have you seen the beard, Tommy?"

"Should be in there"

Bob had a deeper delve into the bag. "No, not here"

"Martin, have you got the beard?" called Tommy.

"No, it's in the bag"

"Apparently not"

"It must be! I saw it in there a few days ago!"

"Not there now" said Bob

"Shit! Where have I put it?!

"He really should be out there by now" said Tommy

"Bit tricky without a beard!" pointed out Bob.

"I'll look out the back!" said Martin rushing off.

"You'll just have to go out there without it" said Tommy.

"I can't!" laughed Bob "the kids are suspicious enough without seeing me in a Santa outfit!

"But there can't be no Santa!"

"There can!" replied Bob, starting to lose some of the Christmas cheer.

Just then, the kitchen door burst open and John from number 87 stumbled in, red in the face from his run to the hall.

"I'm soooo sorry! It was my bloody car, I had to leave it and walk! And my phone was out of charge!"

"It's good to see you John!" Bob smiled with relief as he pulled the robe over his head.

"Only one problem" Bob mentioned "We haven't got a beard!".

John held it up smiling "I took it home last week for its five-yearly wash!"

"Thank Christ for that" smiled Bob.

"You'd better hurry up and get out there!" said Tommy.

"OK, OK" said John pulling on the beard.

Bob opened the door of the kitchen and looked up towards the stage.

"Hold on . . ." The children were already around the stage . . . and there was Father Christmas, sitting in his seat talking to the last of the children.

"I think someone's beaten us to it" smiled Bob.

"What?!" sighed John through his beard. "Who's doing it then?"

"Bloody good outfit" said Martin, looking over Bob's shoulder.

He had certainly been a big hit and the children were very excited.

Father Christmas stood up and surveyed the hall. He smiled through his belly-length beard and rang his golden bell.

"Merry Christmas everyone, Merry Christmas!"

"He's good" said John.

Still waving, Father Christmas picked up his sack and disappeared behind the stage curtains. He still had a lot more to do before the big day and time waited for no-man, not even him.

Blade

Taking the small medieval paper shears onto the flight worried Jack beyond all comprehension and reason. But that's what happens when you're lying in bed trying to sleep with thoughts threatening to distract. So round and round the silly thoughts went, the angel on one shoulder arguing with the demon on the other . . . .

D: "It'll be fine"

A: "But what if it's not? After that terror attack last month, they'll be on high alert . . . "

D: "But it's only a silly little pair of paper scissors!"

A: "It's still a blade though"

D: "It's tiny!"

A: "Big enough to do some damage though"

D: "But who would choose tiny paper scissors as a weapon? I'll leave them separate so it doesn't look like I'm concealing them"

A: "But it's still a pointy blade thing that's banned from flights!"

D: "I've got a razor and that's OK!"

And so it went on . . . way into the small hours.

He'd bought them in a medieval museum on Clover Isle where they had caught his eye, a replica of the medieval originals of course, but nicely forged and beautifully simple. They looked quite innocuous in the shop but now, in his mind they might as well be a big jagged hunting knife. The angel had won and before he left the room for breakfast, he reluctantly left them on the desk for a maid to take, or more likely throw away.

As he sat with his cooked breakfast he sipped coffee from a mug and reflected on his trip. It had been a very restful time in his four days on Clover Isle, just off the Cornish coast, near the Scillies. In many ways it had been stepping back into the 1950's... village shops, Morris Men, maypoles and summer fetes. It reminded him of the "Wicker Man" although thankfully he hadn't noticed any sacrifices!

"It was lovely having you stay with us Mr Telford" smiled the young girl behind the desk at the small hotel "Would you like me to call you a taxi?"

"Yes, that would be great" smiled Jack. Everyone was so friendly on the Island. The complete opposite to the grunting hustle and bustle of London.

After a short wait in reception, his taxi arrived.

"Hello Heather" beamed the thirty-something driver.

"Well hello Mr Briar! It's lovely to see you again"

Even Jack, not the most observant in these matters, could see that they had been more than just friends.

"I'll be seeing you soon" winked Mr Briar.

"That you will!" laughed Heather.

It was a short taxi ride to the airport, crossing sunny rolling green fields.

"Have you enjoyed your visit Mr Telford?" asked the taxi driver in his lilting accent.

"Yes, I have indeed. You are very lucky to live here"

"Oh, we appreciate that sir. We *are* very lucky as you say and we all work hard to keep it this way".

"I hope it never changes!" said Jack.

"Oh I doubt it will. We're far enough off the mainland you see, that they tend to leave us to our own devices"

Jack felt so relaxed that he really wasn't looking forward to returning to the 21st century, but his IT firm beckoned and he'd used up his holiday allowance for the year.

"Thank you" said Jack handing over the very reasonable fare.

"You're welcome" said Mr Briar "We'll see you soon I hope!"

"I'm sure you will" smiled Jack.

Clover Isle Airport was hilarious and reminded Jack more of a shed. At the front of the shed was arrivals with a tiny customs area separating that and the departure gate at the back. And a single shop. It occurred to Jack that you could fit the whole place in a single large shop at Heathrow!

He loved it though and joined the queue of three to check in his suitcase.

"Any of these my love?" the girl asked, pointing towards the poster of banned objects.

"No" he smiled with some confidence, still smarting from leaving the scissors behind.

"That's good then" she smiled "One moment sir". The girl got out of her seat, placed a sticker on Jack's case and after taking two steps, used her radio.

"All good sir, I've just checked and the flight is bang on time"

"Excellent!" smiled Jack.

The rest of the time at the airport was spent as most people would . . . a visit to the toilet (which he rated as "very clean" by pressing the smiley-faced button) a coffee, a snack, and endless glances up at the time which seemed to actually stand still today. Jack liked to be early so he had some time to kill.

The shop was quite something. Small, of course, but with an impressive range of items that Jack wouldn't normally have given a second glance but, because there was nothing else to do, he perused them in some detail. He wasn't sure why as he didn't have anyone to take a gift back to, it was just something to do. He ended up with a bottle of Diet Coke, a small packet of Werther's Originals for the flight (the only time he ever ate them) and a Clover Isle fridge magnet.

"Ladies and gentlemen" crackled over the tannoy "Flight 44 to Southend is now ready to board at Gate 1". Gate 1 was easy to find, being on the left next to Gate 2, the only doors at the back of the shed. The thirty or so, passengers shuffled towards the door, had their boarding passes scanned and walked out onto the hot, shimmering tarmac towards the turbo-prop plane. It had been a while since Jack had been on a plane so small, it holding around 60 passengers.

"Row three sir . . . I think you're on your own in that row today" smiled the hostess.

"Excellent. Thank you" replied Jack, looking forward to the extra space.

The take-off was smooth and Jack watched as tiny Clover Isle revealed itself in all its green glory down below, an emerald laid on a blue velvet sea. Jack watched as the island got smaller and smaller. There was definitely an air of isolation to it.

"Please feel free to take off your seat-belts now" smiled the hostess over the tannoy. Jack clicked his free and opened his Werther's Originals, settling back for the flight.

"Would anybody be interested to join the Captain in the cockpit" said the hostess off of the tannoy, addressing only the first few rows.

Jack loved planes and could think of nothing better. He looked round and no-one else was showing any interest at all, the odd smile but most noses were buried in magazines and sandwiches. He couldn't believe his luck!

"Er, yes I'd like to have a look if that's OK?"

"Of course" she smiled, as if the smile was just for him, and helped him out of his seat.

"Thank you" Jack had a thing for air hostesses that this lady was only reinforcing.

"You are very welcome, Mr . . . ."

"Telford" smiled Jack.

"Yes. Mr Telford!"

"Jack, please"

"Come on in then Jack" she beckoned as she held open the door.

It was bigger than Jack had expected, with a small area behind the pilot and co-pilot, the floor covered in a plastic sheet.

"Mind your footing Mr Telford" warned the hostess. "They're supposed to be laying the new flooring tomorrow, but they said that last week!"

"Ahhh" Jack smiled.

"Mr Telford to join us for a while Captain" smiled the hostess.

"Ah good morning Mr Telford! Very good to see you. Did you enjoy your holiday?"

"Marvellous" replied Jack.

"It gets under your skin doesn't it" said the co-pilot "something magical about it"

"You're right, I'm sorry to be leaving . . . but this is great" said Jack with child-like enthusiasm, trying to take in all the dials and controls.

"You're interested in planes?" asked the Captain.

"Very much" Jack smiled.

"Coffee, Mr Telford?" asked the hostess passing him a mug "It's a bit less formal up here"

"Thank you". Sipping from the mug, Jack tried to take it all in.

"Shall I talk you through the controls?" suggested the Captain.

"Oh, yes please"

The Captain nodded to his co-pilot who took over the helm as the hostess passed The Captain his mug of coffee.

"Right, this here tells us our altitude ... 15,000 ft at the moment. And over here is our horizontal attitude". Jack knew it was a cliché that anyone interested in IT, liked planes and watched "Top Gear" but he fitted the cliché perfectly. He was spellbound as the Captain spent some time carefully describing the controls.

"Well that's about it I think!" smiled the Captain.

"Absolutely fascinating! Thank you!" beamed Jack.

Sipping the last of his coffee from the mug Jack caught sight of a large hunting knife mounted half-way up the wall ...

"Hold on!" smiled Jack, recalling his tiny shears he'd left on the cabinet "I didn't think those were allowed on a flight" he smiled.

"Oh that's only in case we need to cut the seat belts in an emergency" said the hostess taking it off the wall.

"But wouldn't that normally be a covered blade to do that though?"

"Yes, you're right it normally would" said the hostess, plunging the blade into his stomach and pulling it up with some force through his diaphragm.

Jack was wide-eyed as he collapsed to his knees, blood spilling onto the plastic sheeting.

"What? ... " was all he could say.

The hostess said nothing just looked into his eyes and smiled as she held the knife firmly in place.

"Thank you Jack" she whispered as Jack collapsed onto the plastic sheet and took his last breath. She had to use a knife, a gun would be putting the whole plane at risk and, after all, it was tradition. The hostess quickly wrapped Jack in the sheeting, sealing both ends in a fashion as well-rehearsed as the life jacket demonstration.

As the co-pilot banked the plane back towards Clover Isle, the Captain opened the cabin door and presented Jack to the passengers and crew, the red smeared plastic roll cradled in his arms. Everyone stood up and cheered, raising their arms in thanks for the last sacrifice of the season.

It looked like it was going to be another good summer on the Island.

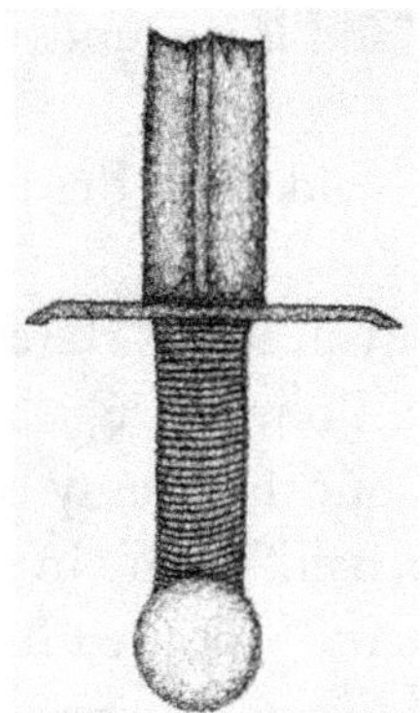

A Wise Investment

Bob had a nose for making money, ever since he was a kid washing cars for 50p. He could smell an opportunity and, at 56, he was smelling one now as his city investment adviser announced across his deep black oak desk: "Now Bob, I have an overseas investment opportunity I'd like to share with you"

"I'm all ears" said Bob, his nose already twitching.

"It'll need some careful positioning and it won't deliver overnight but the returns are very favourable"

"I like the sound of that Gregory" smiled Bob "How favourable?"

"Extremely favourable. In fact, excellent returns are guaranteed!"

"Do me a favour" smiled Bob "Nothing in life is guaranteed!"

"I would agree normally" said Gregory "but this one I will personally underwrite"

"Really!"

"Oh yes, I am *that* confident!"

"Why?" said a suspicious Bob.

"Experience, dear boy. This one is *very* low risk for both of us"

"Seriously" frowned Bob, "a low risk, investment with a guaranteed good return? Sounds too good to be true!"

"I agree" smiled Gregory "and if it sounds like that , it normally *is*, but this really is an exception"

"Well, please do explain" said Bob, the hook now well and truly in his lip.

"Of course, there *is* risk involved . . ." Gregory qualified.

"Ahh, here we go!" smiled Bob, sensing the inevitable catch.

"Actually quite high risk, but the beauty is, in this scheme all the risk is carried by others on our behalf. We are in no way exposed!"

"There's no such investment!!" shouted Bob.

"I can assure you there is! I'm not saying it's easy and it will take some time to realise but I can categorically assure you it *will* work"

"What's the catch then?" asked Bob, knowing there was one.

"Well its not a *small* investment"

"Go on . . ."

Gregory looked Bob straight in the eye "Five billion . . . minimum".

Bob appeared unphased, "Dollars or pounds?"

"Dollars" said Gregory.

"Sounds better and better!" joked Bob.

"I'm definitely interested, but you know what I'm going to ask next"

"Do I?" smiled Gregory "I'm not clairvoyant, dear boy!"

"Why *me* Gregory?" asked Bob looking him straight in the eye "Why *me*?"

"Well you have the funds of course, but more importantly, you have the pedigree, the right connections . . . and the *vision*"

"Ahh, the *vision* . . . it's a new scheme isn't it?!"

"No, no" assured Gregory "Not at all! In fact it's as old as time! Honestly you can't lose"

Bob rocked back in the soft leather chair. He'd worked with Gregory for years and he absolutely trusted his judgement and advice.

"Returns guaranteed you say?" asked Bob.

"*Personally*" confirmed Gregory.

"OK, I'm in for five Gregory. I'll get my people to talk to your people very soon.

"Splendid!" beamed Gregory.

Later that day, Gregory was finally in a position to make the call.

"Hello Home Secretary"

"Ahh, good to hear from you Gregory. I've been expecting your call"

"Now before we continue, Home Secretary . . . I assume it is the same margins this time for weapons and reconstruction projects?"

"Of course", replied the Home Secretary "we see no reason to change the terms of our established contracts"

Gregory smiled. "In that case, I can confirm that the initial funds are indeed in place. We'd like you to start the war as soon as possible please"

"Certainly Gregory, leave it with us" replied the Home Secretary, "You won't be disappointed".

A Time to Die

"I can't tell you the exact time" said the Fortune Teller "but I *can* tell you the day".

Colin was only joking when he asked if he could tell him the day he died.

He was a little light-headed from the hot day and the four beers he had enjoyed that afternoon.

"I thought you guys weren't supposed to tell people that sort of thing, even if you can see it!"

"That is generally true" said the Fortune Teller, looking the part in a golden robe and red turban "but with me, it largely depends who asks".

"Oh" replied Colin rather taken aback. "Go on then, what is it?" the beers asked.

"Are you sure you want to know sir?"

"Yeah, whatever" He didn't believe anything the Fortune Teller had said ... somehow Colin would have found him more convincing if he'd just been wearing a T-shirt and baseball cap.

"Yeah, go on. It'll make planning so much easier!" Colin joked.

Slightly irritated by Colin's attitude, the Fortune Teller simply stated "23rd May 2029"

"You're joking!" said Colin, "That's my birthday!"

"What a happy coincidence" smiled the Fortune Teller.

"So, I'm going to die on my birthday, aged ...." The beer was slowing Colin's calculation.

"68 I believe sir"

"Err yes, that's right, 68!" Colin sat there and pondered this information.

"So you're saying I only have 12 years left?"

"That is correct sir"

"Wow! I'd better get busy planning then" Colin said sarcastically.

"It would be wise sir"

"You know I don't believe you" said Colin directly.

"Yes, I know sir"

"And that doesn't bother you?"

"Not in the slightest sir. I just have access to the information. What you do with it is entirely your concern".

"Ha! You're good you know, the robes and turban and everything"

"I am Nepalese sir. That is what we wear"

"Sure, sure you do! Well how much do I owe you?"

"That will be fifteen pounds sir"

"Fifteen!"

"Yes, I believe that is what we agreed. I can recall information from the past as well as the future" he smiled.

"Ha! You're alright!" smiled Colin, handing over his money.

As he passed the notes across the table, the Fortune Teller grabbed his arm with both hands and looked him straight in the eye.

"Please remember that date sir. I assure you it is accurate"

"Oh I'll remember it!" replied Colin. "Hard to forget isn't it!"

For Colin, it was all a bit of fun, as much of life was.

For reasons obvious to anyone who knew him, Colin didn't have a partner. He liked a girl as much as the next man but he liked a beer and his friends more. Maybe there was a woman who would be content with third place, his lousy manners and body odour, but he hadn't found her yet.

Colin left the Fortune Teller's hut out into the bright sunshine of a Yarmouth afternoon. He had left his best friend Iain drinking on the pier and joined him at around his sixth pint. Colin explained what the Fortune Teller had said.

"And you believe that shite!" laughed Iain.

"No, of course not! Colin pondered for a moment. "He was quite adamant about it though"

"*I'd* be adamant about it for fifteen quid!" laughed Iain, supping his pint. "Mind you, if it's true it could be handy . . ."

"What do you mean?" said Colin.

"Well, technically you could do *anything* and not be killed".

"What are you suggesting?!" laughed Colin "that I should test it?!"

"No but, for argument's sake, you couldn't drown". This was beginning to sound like most conversations they had at the pub.

"No, you're right" agreed Colin "but it could be bloody uncomfortable though!"

They both roared with laughter.

"*And* I'm a first aider" added Iain, "I'd be right there to resuscitate you . . ."

Colin and Iain had tried most things but even *they* weren't stupid enough to try that.

For a year, Colin hadn't given the prediction a lot of thought and his life bowled on much as it always had . . . living in his little flat, working at the laundry, his body odour slightly masked by the smell of dry cleaning chemicals. He was happy in his way with no aspirations to speak of except looking forward to a pint or three with his friend at evenings and weekends. And, after losing his parents, he only had himself to worry about.

However, in August 2018, a day came that would test the Fortune Teller's prediction. A truck squeezed Colin off the motorway slip-road and crushed his car against a concrete wall. He was unconscious in the driving seat when the Fire Service arrived, with both of his legs broken. They were clean breaks at the shins but the jagged car body had cut deep enough that he had lost a lot of blood. In fact there was very little more to lose. With a faint pulse, he was air-lifted to hospital for a transfusion, none of which he could remember. Colin re-joined the world two days later, opening his eyes to two doctors standing over his bed. As he came to, he could hear one of them mumbling about vital signs . . .

"Ahh, Mr Trent! You're back with us!"

Colin went to turn over.

"Please don't try to move Mr Trent, you've had a serious car accident".

"Really?" croaked Colin, not recalling anything and befuddled with morphine.

"Your legs are broken and they're pinned" said the second doctor in a loud South African accent. "Don't worry though, you appear to be doing very well".

"Good" Colin smiled.

"*Good!*" said the first doctor "it's a bona fide *miracle*, that's what it is!"

"Oh?"

"You hardly had a pulse when you arrived"

"And you lost *a lot* of blood at the scene!" added the South African, the doctors now starting to sound like a double act.

"Your heart had nothing left to pump, Mr Trent!" said the first doctor "You should be dead!"

"Eight pints they added!" said the South African "It's a miracle I tell you!"

"Good" repeated Colin falling back to sleep, really fancying a drink.

Iain came to visit Colin later that day, an easy task as he was a nurse in the same hospital.

"Grapes!?" smiled Colin.

"I wasn't sure what to bring" Iain said, visibly shaken.

"They'd better be bloody seedless!" Colin joked holding out his hand. Iain gripped it tightly.

"I thought I'd lost you mate. The doctors reckon you shouldn't be here".

"What do they know" smiled Colin.

"Seriously mate, they told me there was no way to survive what you went through".

"They haven't met my Fortune Teller have they" Colin smiled.

"You know what" said Iain with tears in his eyes, "I'm beginning to think there's something in that"

"Made me think" nodded Colin "Maybe we *do* all have a time?"

"We need time for a drink, that's for sure!" said Iain, breaking the melancholy.

"Not this week, but I'll sneak you in a pint soon mate" whispered Iain "I promise".

It would be three weeks before Colin was released from hospital but his recovery was quick and by the last week, he was feeling surprisingly well. Well enough for a bedside visit from the local newspaper. He even made the front page: "The Man Who Wouldn't Die!" was the headline and he became a minor local celebrity. Colin hadn't mentioned the Fortune Teller for fear of being seen as a crank, but during the whole episode, the words of the Fortune Teller had rolled around his head. "Don't be ridiculous" Colin told himself "It *can't* be true!"

After a couple of months, other stories started to catch peoples' eye and Colin's short-lived fame began to wane with life following it's old familiar patterns.

"Of course, I could have just been bloody lucky" said Colin passing Iain the crisps at the pub.

"Mate" said Iain earnestly "you shouldn't be here! I don't know what the docs said to you, but they were straight with me. Apparently you're a walking dead man!"

"Mmm . . . makes you think doesn't it" said Colin.

"Are you thinking what I'm thinking?" smiled Iain.

"You know I am!" smiled Colin, their thoughts often coinciding.

"It's a bit weird though" said Iain "even for us".

"What, thinking of different ways of trying to kill yourself and cheat death?! I don't know what you mean!"

Their thoughts had often been in tune and often they were odd, but this one ranked high in the oddness stakes.

"Hanging is out" stated Colin.

"Yes, way too painful in the recovery" agreed Iain "but perhaps a poisoning of some sort . . ."

"I'd been thinking the same" said Colin "just to test it out"

"There's a compound at the hospital that they have to carry an antidote for . . ." said Iain deep in thought.

"Go on . . ." said Colin firmly on the hook.

"Well it would be easy to lay my hands on both. *And* it's a narcotic effect, so you'd feel great during the experiment!"

"*Experiment!*" laughed Colin "I'm not a lab rat!"

"You know what I mean, I'm not going to let you die! I could bring you back instantly at any point. But if I slowly give you a dose that, without the antidote, would be 100% fatal, that *is* going to prove a point"

"Oh great!" said Colin

"Seriously, it's *totally* controllable. I'm not about to kill my best friend!"

Colin was reckless by nature, beyond reason at times but this was a risky move even for him. However, one thing sealed the decision . . . his total faith in Iain.

"I suppose we've all got to die of something!" Colin joked.

"I'm not treating it as a joke mate, it's a sure-fire way of testing if you're actually death-proof!"

"And you're *sure* about the risk?" said Colin.

"Never been surer about anything! I've used it a lot and watched it being used for years"

Colin didn't need much thinking time. "Fuck it, let's do it!"

"I've got it!" said Iain furtively down the phone.

"Tonight then?" asked Colin.

"Yeah, that's fine with me". Colin was feeling good, partly down to ignorance but also in large part due to his total trust in his friend. On paper it was lunacy, to say nothing of illegal, but for these two it was just another adventure. If it worked it would be proof, if proof were needed after Colin's last experience. Later that evening, on Colin's kitchen table, Iain laid out the tools of his trade. Antiseptic swabs, sterile needles, syringe and a small brown bottle of the drug that Iain had prepared at home.

"How the hell do you get this stuff out?!" said Colin.

"It's not the first time" said Iain preparing the syringe. Colin knew it wasn't.

"Ready?" asked Iain.

"Born ready" joked Colin, masking a 20% trepidation. Colin's increased heart rate meant that a prominent vein was easy for Iain to find.

"Here we go then. If you feel weird as this is going in, let me know and I'll stop and deliver the antidote"

"OK"

Iain slowly squeezed the liquid into Colin's arm. Almost immediately Colin smiled the silliest smile.

"Wooow . . . where did you get *this* stuff from!" It wasn't Colin's first drug experience, far from it, but it was the best by a country mile.

"Keep going" Colin grinned.

"OK". Iain knew he was nearing the dose that would be a problem.

"*Oh my God . . .*" said Colin, eyes rolling into his head.

"Still good?" asked Iain.

"Mmm" replied Colin with a smile so fixed he felt it would never leave.

Iain pushed the remainder of the liquid in knowing that, by now, Colin should be in serious trouble.

"You've got to get us some more of this" Colin whispered.

Iain checked his vital signs and they were all good. "How do you feel?".

"I feel . . . everything. *Everything!*" Colin shouted, trying to stand up.

"Woah there tiger! Best you stay seated!" Iain had expected Colin to display more of the undesirable symptoms: depression of the respiratory system, tremors, but all he seemed to feel was pleasure. Apart from a slightly elevated heart rate and flushed complexion he seemed fine! Iain couldn't believe it! Again, his friend was a walking, talking dead man!

The next day, all signs of the drug metabolised out of his system, Colin and Iain looked at each other across the pub table.

"That's *twice*" said Iain looking Colin straight in the eye.

"Yeah" smiled Colin.

"It's looking like that bloody Fortune Teller was right! said Iain.

"It really does! I actually know when I'm going to die! Twenty-third of May 2029 !" Colin wasn't entirely sure this was a good or bad thing. They both supped their beers deep in thought for a couple of minutes.

"Of course, you know we could make some money out of this don't you" said Iain. He could almost hear the penny drop in Colin's mind.

"Jesus, I guess we could! You mean some kind of . . . public demonstration?"

"Exactly! We could reproduce what we've just done, or something similar. Get some newspapers involved?"

"Do you think they'd be interested?" asked Colin.

"You're kidding!" laughed Iain "They'd lap it up! Leave it with me, I know someone who knows someone . . . "

"You always do!" smiled Colin.

Iain's contact with the newspaper started a series of events that neither of the boys could have ever predicted. The paper's sister TV company saw the story and thought it was ideal for a live broadcast on one of their stations. And they were prepared to pay handsomely for the privilege. The boys were to appear on the show "How do they do that?", a collection of escapologists, contortionists and acts bordering on sideshow freaks.

The boys loved the show and the TV company thought Colin and Iain were a perfect fit. When they talked of repeating the administration of the drug live on TV, the lawyers were hesitant but, after some wrangling they managed to organise it, this time legally and with a team of medics standing by. There was never a point in the discussions when the boys didn't feel completely confident and on the night, everything went *exactly* to plan with Colin enjoying another very pleasant drugs trip. The only difference this time was he was being paid handsomely for it! The audience loved it and no-one could figure it out, the medics completely dumbfounded. They knew the drug was administered and he should be dead.

Their "act" soon became an internet sensation, making them both even more money. The boys were over the moon but despite the success, an underlying public suspicion developed that it *must* be some kind of trick or illusion. "It had to be or he'd be dead!" No-one could figure it out but it seemed no-one thought it was anything more than an act.

The exercise was so lucrative that the boys could have stopped there and then and never needed to work again, but that wasn't Colin and Iain's style. So they decided to up the stakes . . .

Two months earlier, egged on by alcohol, they had already tried a closely monitored drowning and had discovered it really wasn't a painful experience. Colin could feel a strange chill as his lungs filled with water and then he just fell asleep, until Iain pressed his chest a few times, placed him on his side and emptied his lungs. Colin then regained consciousness, seemingly unaware of the whole event. So they organised a live drowning/revival on the show. Some commentators reported on the poor taste of the whole affair, but that didn't stop the boys . . . they knew it would work! And it did. Everything went perfectly to plan, Colin being successfully revived with minimal discomfort in front of another huge live audience.

"Jesus, we are onto a goldmine here, Col!" whispered Iain to Colin on stage as they smiled and took the applause.

However, it didn't take long for the voices of the naysayers to start to be heard over the believers . . .

"He just *survived!*"

"He drowned and he was lucky to be revived! That's not unique!"

"Where's the entertainment in *that*?!"

The boys still couldn't seem to get away from the fact that most people believed these were elaborate tricks. It didn't take that long before peoples' attention turned to the next sensation, with Colin and Iain slipping back into relative obscurity. Not that this bothered the boys at all . . . The internet revenue was fairly consistent and they had amassed more money than they had ever dreamed of. With this rise to wealth being so public, the TV company had warned them that they may be approached by various parties trying to make a claim and, inevitably it happened. And the boys ignored them all ... requests from old work colleagues who had fallen on "hard times", the charity approaches and the genuinely needy. They simply employed an agent to deal with them and politely declined, sometimes not so politely. They knew what it was like not to have much money but they felt this was *their* time now and they had earned it. *They* had taken the risks so *they* should reap the rewards. After all, Colin had to live with the fact that he knew when he was going to die! Not that this bothered him at all, he was living the dream. Colin's favourite approach was from a charity working with Ebola in Sierra Leone ... would he be interested in helping them as he couldn't be killed by the disease?!

"Bloody cheek!" said Colin, "It might not kill me but it could be bloody unpleasant bleeding from every orifice!"

"Maybe not" said Iain "drowning was like falling asleep for you and being poisoned was a perfect high!"

"There's no way they're getting me out there!" said Colin.

Sometimes knowing when you are going to die can be a big advantage. Colin had employed financial advisers to release his new-found wealth in a controlled way. He had no-one to leave it to and wanted to spend every penny before he went. Ideally, he'd be spending the last of his money on a pint as he drew his last breath.

"Shame everyone can't know their date" thought Colin "Makes life so much easier".

Four years passed and life had been very good to Colin. One day, quite by chance he found himself back in Great Yarmouth not far from the pier and he found himself wondering if the same Fortune Teller might still be there ...

His driver stopped at the pier entrance and he could see that the hut was still there. Yes, that was it!

"Wait here, I won't be long" said Colin. The day was overcast and the pier quite quiet for early Summer as he strolled up the pier, glimpses of brown waves beneath the planks. When he reached the hut the weathered red door was slightly ajar ... he knocked and tentatively shouted "Hello!"

"Can I help you?" said the Fortune Teller. He was still dressed in the golden robe and red turban and didn't look a day older than the last time Colin saw him. But Colin figured he looked pretty old then.

"You probably don't remember me but I visited you about . . . "

"Eight years ago" smiled the Fortune Teller.

"Yes, it was about that . . . " smiled Colin.

"Indeed, I remember you well sir".

"You might remember, you told me the date that I'd die"

"Oh yes, I remember sir. I have only ever told three people that".

"Oh" said Colin taken slightly aback "Well, it seems, you might be right about the date . . . so far at least!".

"I have every reason to believe it is right sir. I saw you on that show you know" smiled the Fortune Teller smoothing out the green velvet table cloth with his hands. "I know it was no illusion".

"You're the only one who doesn't think it was a cheap trick!" smiled Colin.

"No trick sir, just the way of the natural world" said the Fortune Teller.

"Am I being charged for this?" joked Colin.

"Only if you sit down sir"

"OK" smiled Colin sitting down.

The Fortune Teller was surprised "What more do you need to know sir, life is good for you isn't it?"

"It certainly is!" replied Colin "Is it still fifteen pounds?"

"You have a good memory sir" smiled the Fortune Teller "Actually it is twenty now"

Colin reached into his wallet and passed over two £10 notes.

Without touching the notes, the Fortune Teller smiled and held Colin's hand. For a few moments nothing was said. The Fortune Teller then placed his other palm on top of the hand he was holding.

"You must make the most of each day sir, it's later than you think"

Colin roared with laughter "Is that all I get for £20!"

"Yes sir, I think that is it. But you are right sir, don't worry about the money" said the Fortune Teller sliding it back across the tablecloth.

"Sweet!" smiled Colin.

"Good day to you sir" smiled the Fortune Teller "and take care".

On the morning it happened, Colin had a real spring in his step. Life was good and he was feeling it as he hopped down the last of the spiral stairs. As his socked foot hit the polished hardwood floor, the chances of any grip were always going to be minimal. He went down so quickly he had no time to react, the back of his head striking the edge of the second step so hard that unconciousness was instant. When he woke up in hospital, he could see Iain in his nurse's uniform slowly come into focus.

"Hello mate" said Iain, tears rolling down his cheeks. Good old Iain. Colin would always have Iain. The fall had left him completely paralysed from the neck down but still very much alive. Colin was sixty-one and he knew he would live for another seven years. He didn't want to but, by now, he absolutely knew he would.

R.I.P Bobby

"Where's Bobby Mum?" said little Madelaine from the front seat of the car, concerned that Bobby the goat was nowhere to be seen.

Madelaine's Mum, Jenny read the sign and was shocked.

"Oh dear" she said "It looks like Bobby might not be here anymore"

They drove on in silence, a silence that quite surprised Jenny. Bobby had *always* been there. Every journey to school down that country lane as they passed the farm, Bobby the goat would be tied by a rope to his small wooden hut. All through Summer, all through Winter there would be Bobby, munching grass from the wide verge in front of the hut bearing his name above the entrance, looking for all the world like a large dog kennel. All the children knew Bobby. Most of the adults knew Bobby too, saying hello and waving as they drove past.

The sign above Bobby's kennel now read "R.I.P Bobby x"

"What does R.I.P mean Mummy?" Madelaine was eight now but hadn't come across that expression.

"Oh, I'm afraid it means Rest in Peace, Maddy" said her mother directly, never one to shield Madelaine from the truth. "I think something may have happened to him and he has died dear"

Madelaine sniffled in her seat. She understood. She had lost gerbils when she was six and her mother had explained then.

"Poor Bobby. I'm going to miss him" sniffed Madelaine.

"I'll miss him too" agreed Jenny with a tear in her eye. All the years they had passed in the car to and from school, they had never once stopped to pet the goat or have a closer look. Bobby was just *there*, he'd always been there and that had been his place, for some reason making everybody smile as they passed.

When Madelaine got to school, many of her friends who travelled on the same road had noticed the sign too. "Did you see that little Bobby was dead?" asked her friend with red eyes and damp cheeks. As she held her hand, Madelaine was pleased she'd got the initial shock out of her system with her Mum. It hadn't helped her friend when one of the boys had pointed out to her that you can make a good curry out of goats… "They've probably eaten him by now!" he laughed. Yes, Bobby had certainly made an impact, probably way beyond that of most goats in the county with most of Madelaine's friends being visibly subdued that morning.

That evening, Madelaine snuggled down in her bedsheets, their familiar smell a comfort after her unsettling day.

"I've been thinking Mum"

"Careful, that could become a habit" her mother smiled.

"Why did they keep Bobby tied to the kennel on the verge like that?"

"Probably because he was so close to that road" Jenny said stroking her daughter's forehead. "You have to remember we only saw him twice a day".

"Maybe he liked seeing us and all the cars" said Madelaine.

"I'm sure he did, everybody waving to him! How many goats have *that* every morning and evening?!"

Madelaine smiled. "Can we talk to the people in the farm?"

"Ah, I'm not sure about that Maddy" said Jenny, having never seen the owner.

"Can't we just call and say we're sorry?" said Madelaine looking up, eyes wide. Jenny was reluctant to agree but then thought "What harm could it do? Might even help Maddy".

"OK Maddy, we will. We'll knock on the farmer's door tomorrow morning if you like".

Madelaine beamed "Thanks Mum!"

"Now get some sleep young lady" said her mother, kissing her daughter on the cheek. "Sleep tight, and don't let the bed bugs bite!" Madelaine closed her eyes feeling better than she had all day.

On Saturday morning, they headed out to the farm as Madelaine's mother had promised, down the long familiar country lane. Jenny parked the car up on the wide grass verge and they slowly walked over to Bobby's kennel for the first time.

His rope lay coiled on the ground, no longer being pulled and dragged, just motionless. They both quietly looked at the sign. "They must have really liked him" said Jenny holding Madelaine's hand. Mother and daughter walked onto the stone path that led up to the small farmhouse to the right of the barn. The old stone house wouldn't be picked to feature on any postcard but it had a certain working quaintness about it. Jenny looked down at her daughter and knocked on the small oak door, hoping an angry farmer wouldn't open it with a shotgun. It didn't take long for Mrs McAleer to open it. And fortunately she was unarmed.

"Good morning to you" she smiled in her broad Southern Irish accent.

"Hello" said Jenny "I'm sorry to disturb you but we couldn't help noticing that Bobby had gone and my daughter really wanted to say she was sorry".

Mrs McAleer wasn't much taller than Madelaine and could see the sorrow in the little girl's eyes.

"Ahh, that's really good of you both" she said, genuinely touched. "We all miss him you know. He was part of the family so he was. Now would you come in and have a cup of tea with me?"

"We should really be going" said Jenny reluctant to impose but she could see her smiling daughter was keen.

"You'd be keeping an old lady company" Mrs McAleer added, smiling back to Madelaine.

"If you're sure?" said Jenny.

"Absolutely! I've got some cake too if you'd like"

Mrs McAleer settled her visitors into her large old kitchen.

"My son is out on the farm at the moment and he'll not be back for an hour or two". As Mrs McAleer poured tea from a huge brown pot, Jenny explained how Bobby had become a minor celebrity among the children and parents of the school.

"Oh yes" smiled Mrs McAleer "It's *always* been like that . . . he really was a bonny goat!" Madelaine could see that she cared a lot for Bobby.

"Och it was a horrible to-do . . . he was hit by a car you know".

Maddy's eyes started to brim.

"But don't you be too upset now!" interrupted Mrs McAleer "he was 137!"

"Really?!" said Maddy wide-eyed.

"Oh yes, *really*!" replied Mrs McAleer winking to Maddy's Mum.

Mrs McAleer slid a plate with a big slice of Victoria sponge towards Madelaine.

"Now you make a start on that and I can tell you all about it if you like?"

Madelaine nodded.

"Now my husband was a clever man when he was alive.. God rest his soul" She made the sign of the cross on her chest.

"Oh yes, he was clever, A *scientist* you know . . . and one day, in his shed at the bottom of the garden he made a *potion!*" (she thought that potion would sound more exotic to Madelaine than chemical). Maddy's eyes widened. Her Mum smiled.

"And this potion had magical powers"

"Magic?" said Madelaine, a full mouth of cake muffling her words.

"Oh, I know it sounds unlikely" said Mrs McAleer "but like I said, he was a clever man. Anyway, he tried out this potion on some of our goats"

Madelaine nodded. "What happened?"

"Well, I'll tell you what happened, young lady . . . nothing".

Madelaine smiled.

"Nothing at all!" laughed Mrs MacAleer. Jenny laughed, loving her natural Irish story-telling.

"I gave him some stick so I did! Weeks in the shed he was, with this potion and for what! Nothing! Until about a couple of years later, we noticed something . . . ."

"What?" said Madeline through her second mouthful.

Well, we noticed that Bobby didn't seem to be getting any older!" Mrs McAleer winked to Jenny.

Madelaine's mouth opened, crumbs stuck to her tongue.

"First we thought he was just a bit fitter than the rest of them, but after a few years Bobby just hadn't changed. The potion had kept him the same age!"

"Wow" said Madelaine.

"So you see he should have only lived for about 12 years or so, but he actually lived 137 years in all! Can you believe that!"

Madelaine shook her head.

"That's why *I* can remember Bobby, my Mum can remember Bobby and *lots and lots* of people can remember him, because he lived *10 times* longer than a goat should!"

Madelaine loved this thought and smiled.

"Not just that, but what a life he led! He liked to sleep and eat in his little hut out the front so we'd tie him up so he wouldn't wander, but most of the day he'd play and jump in the field out the back and get spoilt by the children. Ahh, he had a grand life so he did!"

Maddy felt a lot better about the whole thing.

"And you know he's still with us in spirit, looking down on us from goat heaven so he is!"

"*Goat heaven!* She's good!" thought Jenny eating her cake. She liked Mrs McAleer a lot and thought this wouldn't be the last time she would drop in.

"*Goat heaven?*" asked Madelaine, "Is it just goats there?"

"Of course!" replied Mrs McAleer "if they had wolves there as well there'd be hell to pay wouldn't there"

Madelaine laughed.

Jenny and her daughter grinned as they finished their tea and cake, chatting for a while longer with Mrs McAleer.

"Thank you sooo much" Jenny whispered as they left "you've really helped her."

"Ooch, tis nothing!" Mrs McAleer smiled "it was lovely to chat to you both and I'm glad of the company! You make sure you call again now!"

"Thank you, we will!" smiled Jenny, walking back up the path, with a feeling that she had found a new friend.

After preparing lunch for her son, Mrs McAleer brought her fourth pot of tea out into the garden to enjoy the sunshine. She set her cup and saucer on the table and browsed through a magazine in the sun before the work of the afternoon. She'd been reading that drinking too much tea and coffee is apparently not that good for you, but she wasn't unduly worried. She had taken Mr McAleer's potion when she was 47. At 161 she looked good on it and Mrs McAleer figured she had a good few years left.

Door B

Apart from the busier-than-usual traffic on their way to the airport, Pauline and Jim's journey to departure gate B42 at Heathrow had been remarkably stress-free. Even the Louisiana Cajun Bean sandwiches they had just eaten actually tasted of something quite close to Louisiana Cajun Beans. Earlier, they had strolled straight through an almost empty check-in hall, up to an almost non-existent queue. Even the nightmare that normally is "security" had been a breeze. No corralling into an endless zig-zagging queue, no bored Border Officer moaning at people for not removing their laptops from their hand luggage . . . just a calm, pleasant efficiency. Pauline had even smiled as she zipped up her boots and reunited her wrist with her watch. Yes, it had been a smooth passage and they were both surprisingly relaxed as they stood by departure gate B42.

"I've got some sweets for the take-off and landing" said Pauline.

"Excellent! Let's break them out now!" replied Jim, not blessed with patience.

"No, they're for the flight!"

The tannoy barked an interruption: *"We would now like to invite passengers from rows 24 to 36 to embark. Please have your passports open on the photo page and your boarding passes ready. Thank you"*

Pauline and Jim were row 25.

"First to board as well! This day is just getting better and better!" said Jim. The couple approached the desk and were greeted by a smart young hostess.

Smiling, she looked at their passports very carefully, holding them up to their faces for comparison. Jim had a flutter of concern as he'd grown a short beard since the picture had been taken. "Just to make you look more like a terrorist" Pauline had joked earlier.

"Thank you and have a pleasant flight" smiled the hostess, "Oh, and you need Door A as you go through, on the left".

"Thank you" smiled Jim, slightly distracted by her prettiness.

As they walked down the broad, bright corridor, there seemed to be a hold-up behind them.

"It's like we've got the place to ourselves today" said Jim, "Shall I take your passport?"

"No, that's fine"

"I'll take it, to keep them together" pressed Jim, preferring to know they're safe.

"Sure". Pauline handed it over, knowing it would annoy him until he had them together.

"I'll have one of those sweets too!" smiled Jim.

"Honestly, it's like taking a child away!"

On their left above a large white door was a large rectangular yellow sign "Door A" and a few steps down, a similarly large sign indicating "Door B". Jim could see through the glazed wall that they led to the plane via the usual raised interconnecting tunnel.

"Damn! Did she say Door A or Door B?" said Jim.

"Not sure" said Pauline looking back up the empty corridor for some fellow passengers to ask.

"Pretty sure it was B" said Jim.

"Really?" doubted Pauline.

"No, it was definitely B" said Jim with some commitment. Still no-one approached up the corridor.

"Yes, I'm sure it was" said Jim impatiently.

"There's no rush is there?" said Pauline.

"I guess not" replied Jim, unconvinced.

"Someone will be along soon and we'll ask them" assured Pauline.

A long minute passed and still no-one appeared.

"We're not in the wrong corridor are we?" asked Jim.

"No, I'm pretty sure this was the only way. I'll go back and ask"

"No don't worry, I'm *sure* it's Door B" said Jim, walking over to open it.

"This is the exciting bit isn't it" smiled Jim as he walked through the door, "The final tunnel onto the plane!"

"I suppose so" said Pauline, still doubting the choice of door as it clicked shut behind them. Considerably smaller than the corridor, the tunnel was very well-lit, it's clinically white walls dotted with colourful posters advertising exotic destinations. They walked down towards a slight bend in the tunnel.

"Where's everyone else?" said Pauline, concerned.

"I don't know but we should get on the plane and wait in our seats. They'll be along! They won't want to miss the flight!"

Pauline's mood wasn't quite so jocular. "I'm not sure about this" said Pauline turning back to the door to open it. It was locked shut.

"Oh great, now we're bloody locked in! Why can't you wait *5 minutes!*" she snapped.

"It'll be fine" reassured Jim "someone will be along any moment. Let's go down and ask"

"OK" said Pauline unconvinced.

They turned the bend in the tunnel and looked down the gently sloping floor to the end where you'd expect the usual concertina attachment to the plane.

"What?" Pauline looked towards the end and was faced with closed doors with a young man sitting down on a chair in front of them. That in itself was unusual but the fact that he was dressed in a clown's outfit she really didn't expect. Jim looked at Pauline and then back at the Clown. "Is the plane ready to board yet?" he asked, not believing he had casually asked this of a clown.

"Not quite sir" said the Clown not looking up from the clipboard on his lap.

"Where's everyone else?" asked Pauline.

"Oh outside I'd expect" smiled the Clown looking up from the board, "you were just a bit keen to come in. That's why I'm here. Can I see your boarding passes please?"

"No!" shouted Pauline "I want to see your manager!"

"Oh good luck" laughed the Clown, "So do I! She let's me do my own thing these days. You could say we had a little falling out"

"I'm not bloody interested in your boss!" shouted Jim, "We have a plane to catch!"

"Please sir in good time. If you would let me finish … as I say we had a little *falling out*" the Clown smiled, *"she fell out of a building! Ha, ha, ha!"* The clown cackled with laughter, tears running down his made-up face.

"I'm so sorry" said the Clown composing himself "It's no joke being lost is it. Now, didn't the lady say Door *A* to you? I think that she probably *did* say Door *A,* didn't she."

"I told you it was *A*!!" shouted Pauline.

"Don't have a go at me!" snapped Jim "we're talking to a bloody clown!"

"Not to worry, not to worry" smiled the Clown "We'll sort it out one way or the other. It's just they normally *do* say Door *A,* quite specifically"

"Well can you let us out and we'll get to Door A?" asked Pauline "The flight is due to leave in 10 minutes!"

"About seven actually!" laughed the Clown looking at his wristwatch, "but don't worry about that just now"

"What do you mean? We need to be *on* that flight!"

"*Need* to be on it?! *Need* to be on it?! I *need* to breathe! I *need* to sleep! I don't think I need to fly! Ha, ha!"

"OK, I've had just about enough of this nonsense" said Pauline.

"Forgive me for saying so" interrupted the Clown, "but most people do tend to expect a little nonsense from a clown! In fact, I find people can be quite disappointed if there *isn't* some nonsense!" he laughed.

"Will you shut the fuck up!" screamed Pauline "We need to catch that bloody flight!!"

"Well, if you'd listened" said the Clown straight-faced, "I think you'll find that it really isn't that important in the scheme of things. Trust me"

Pauline didn't.

"Now if we can all calm down, I'll take your flight numbers please"

"You know what bloody flight we're on it's just over there!" shouted Jim.

"Sir, the quicker we do this, the quicker we can all get on"

"It's FB704" said Pauline dead pan, remembering the number from the information boards.

"F-B-7-0-4" repeated the Clown carefully entering the number in the sheet on his clipboard.

"And is it the same number for you sir?"

"No, I booked a separate flight from my wife just for a change!!"

"Now there's no need for sarcasm sir. It's the lowest form of wit they say"

"OK, F-B-7-0-4" said the clown entering the flight number.

"And your passenger reference numbers please"

"Oh for Christ's sake we are going to miss that plane!" shouted Jim.

"Just give it to him Jim" said Pauline calmly.

Fuming, Jim fumbled for the print-outs in his rucksack.

"OK, Mine is 34728FG and my wife's is 34727FG"

"Thank you, smiled the Clown "now that wasn't too difficult was it?"

Pauline raised her hand to hold Jim back.

"3-4-7-2-8-F-G and 3-4-7-2-7-F-G" said the Clown slowly entering the numbers "Excellent!"

The Clown then looked up and, with a broad smile and looking Jim directly in the eye, slowly tore the sheet in two and screwed it up, laughing hysterically as he threw it behind him.

"What the hell do you think you are doing?!" shouted Jim.

"I told you!" roared the Clown, "it's not really that important!"

"I've had enough of this!" Jim ran up the slight slope back to the door.

"It was still firmly locked. He started banging on it.

"Please sir, you are wasting your time with that" shouted the Clown still seated. "I'd hate you to hurt yourself" he shouted unconvincingly. *"Before me"* he smiled under his breath.

"What was that?" said Pauline.

"Oh your young hearing is *excellent* Madam, *excellent!*

Pauline was open-mouthed and fear started to rise from her belly.

Then, like a train, it hit her.

"We're not getting out of here are we" said Pauline.

"I'm afraid not" smiled the Clown.

Every Breath You Take

Ed liked to dampen his thumb and press up the last crumbs of the crisps from the foil packet. It was more of a habit rather than a desire to get his full money's worth. To take away the saltiness, he sipped the froth off his pale ale and continued his conversation with his good friend, Liam.

"I've been thinking" said Ed.

"That's where you're going wrong" joked Liam "It's thinking that's got the world into the state it is now!"

"You're absolutely right of course!" smiled Ed. "Because of people bloody thinking, we've got the internet, wars, religion, day-time TV . . . all manner of distractions to our core activity"

"What, talking rubbish down the pub with a pint and crisps?"

"Exactly! Anything that detracts from our core activity, our *mission* indeed, needs to be shunned and possibly punished"

"Punished? Bit harsh!"

"Is it though? How else are we going to stop it?"

"You make a good point! Are we talking hanging or a Chinese burn here?"

"A range, Liam, a range, depending on how deeply people are thinking. A passing thought might warrant a Chinese burn but if people really start putting their minds to it ... religious dilemmas, cancer cures and the like ... then we'll have to come in a bit more heavy-handed"

"To get the message across" Liam nodded.

"Of course, how are we going to stop it otherwise?!"

Smiling they both sipped their pints. About once a week, for an hour or so, they would do exactly the same, visit the pub, have a pint with crisps and talk nonsense. The nonsense could easily go on for hours. It flowed naturally, much to the annoyance of their wives when they were all together, who quite quickly reached the point when it started not to be quite so funny ... irritating even. Fortunately, Ed and Liam never tired of it.

The themes were similar: the fact that Ed always seemed to eat all the crisps; the on-going argument about who had a more working-class upbringing (in truth they both did, but Liam insisted that having a pet rabbit was middle-class while Ed asserted that only middle-upper class subjects had balconies like his old council flat had. "Even the Queen has a balcony!" he pointed out).

"Anyway, like I was saying before I was rudely interrupted, I've been thinking"

"Yeah, you said" said Liam pausing for a sip "I suppose you're going to tell me what it was about?"

"Not, if you don't want me to!" said Ed, feigning offence.

"Of course I want you to, you fool. I can't *wait* to hear what you have been *personally* thinking!" replied Liam sarcastically.

"Well maybe I won't tell you!"

"Good! You and your *thinking!*" laughed Liam.

There was a pause. "Go on then, what were you thinking?"

"Oh, you want to know now do you?!" joked Ed.

"Maybe I do, maybe I don't ... "

"Well I'm going to bloody tell you anyway whether you like it or not!"

"Go on then" smiled Liam.

"I've been thinking" said Ed, "that *breathing* is the weirdest thing".

It was a bit of a showstopper for Liam.

"Err, I suppose so. I haven't really thought about it" .

"Well it's lucky for you I *have* then!" smiled Ed. "Seriously though, they slap you on your backside when you're born and you gulp in that first gasp of air, and from then on, it's continual breathing until you snuff it!

In and out, in and out, while you're awake, even while you're asleep . . . in and out, on and on it goes, never having to think about it!"

"Well I'm going to have to take issue with you there" pointed out Liam.

"I used to see how long I could hold my breath underwater as a kid, so it's not really *continuous* is it?"

"Good point, well made, but you didn't stop for long did you?"

"No, I didn't" Liam agreed.

"Sure there's the odd hiccup" said Ed, " . . . a sneeze, a cough, a deep breath taken to blow your birthday candles out but, by and large, it's just this non-stop wave of breathing until you die!".

"What's your point here mate?" asked Liam with a sip.

"Don't you find it *odd?*"

"I find it odd that you've eaten all the snacks again! Shall I get some nuts?"

Liam restocked the drinks and furnished them with two packets of dry roasted peanuts.

"Ooh, dry roasted!" said Ed, opening them before they hit the table.

"Seriously though" said Ed "don't you find this breathing thing odd?"

"Sure it's a bit odd" agreed Liam "but it's pretty standard for us mammals. It's what we do!"

"Don't get me wrong" said Ed, "I'm not complaining, I just find it weird that all of our lives it carries on"

"Like your heartbeat of course" observed Liam.

"Indeed" agreed Ed, "I suppose it doesn't do to dwell on these things too much. Just be thankful they *do* carry on"

"It really *would* be irritating if breathing was a conscious effort, wouldn't it!" said Liam. Ed burst out laughing, spraying three nuts across the table.

"Can you imagine" said Liam, "In, out, in . . . Oh I must remember to call John on Thursday, out . . . in, out . . . what was it I wanted from the shops? . . . *IN!*"

With the timing of a comedian, Liam's comment really hit Ed's funny bone.

He laughed uncontrollably, his mouth wide open displaying the half crunched nuts.

"It wasn't that funny" said Liam dead pan, which didn't help Ed who found it even more hilarious. His next involuntary suck of breath took some nuts with it and they lodged at the back of his throat.

"Careful, you'll do yourself a mischief!" laughed Liam as Ed turned a brighter red. Ed wasn't laughing now. Holding his throat, he couldn't breath in at all.

"Shit! Are you OK mate?"

Ed's face was bright red as he tried in vain to breath in. He stood up and started to panic, knocking their drinks off the table. He really had to think about his next breath now, the mushy cake of peanuts blocking his windpipe completely. Now it was all he could think about in the world . . . what was once so easy was now impossible. Why couldn't he just fucking breath in?! His face burned and his head buzzed as he started to lose conciousness . . . Liam slapped him as hard as he could on the back. It made no difference, Ed by now a beetroot purple, doubled up in writhing panic. From nowhere, the barman appeared, pushing the table aside and from behind Ed, he put his arms around his belly and performed a perfect Heimlich manoeuvre, peanuts once again spraying across the table. Ed inhaled, the loudest, sweetest, coolest breath, straightening him up as the air rushed in. As he breathed out he could feel his head stop buzzing as he returned to the room. He was hesitant to breathe in again for fear of another restriction but the second breath was almost as good as the first and the beetroot drained from his face as he slumped back down into the Chesterfield chair.

"That's the third time I've used that" said the barman "works like a charm!"

"Thank you" wheezed Ed holding the barman's hand, grateful for the simple pleasure of breathing again.

"Are you sure you're OK?" said Liam in shock, the floor strewn with glasses and peanuts.

"Yeah, I'm good now" nodded Ed, snorting in another breath.

"You know, I've been thinking" said Ed, his breathing almost back to normal.

"Oh God, what now!"

"I think I'll stick to crisps in future".

El Poncho

"Now you don't see that every day!" Peter said to his daughter as they sat in the car waiting at the traffic lights. In front of them, a tousled grey-haired man was casually crossing the busy dual-carriageway, strolling across the central reservation. People often sneaked across there, so there was nothing unusual in that. What *was* unusual was that he was dressed in a cowboy hat and a multi-coloured poncho, with a small guitar slung across his back, looking for all the world like a minstrel who had just finished rounding up his horses in Peru, prior to accompanying himself on a set of pan pipes. He strolled across the road with a smile and a casual gait that suggested he was entirely comfortable with his surroundings, even though his surroundings were not entirely comfortable with him. He then stopped at the "no waiting sign" to Peter's left. He turned to Peter, looked him straight in the eye, reached up and wrote a big "X" across the sign with his index finger, his action leaving no mark on the sign. He then beamed a smile and continued his long-legged gait across the grass verge onto the footpath.

"What the hell?!" said Bridget, Peter's daughter "Do you know him?".

"No" said Peter open-mouthed as the light turned green and they had to move.

"Follow him dad, follow him!"

"We can't, we've got stuff to do!"

"Not any more we haven't" said Bridget "I can get the stationery anytime"

"OK" said Peter crawling away. It was hard to go slow enough to keep tabs on him but by turning left a couple of times they managed to back-track a little. He seemed to be slowly heading towards the Town Centre with no particular urgency. Every now and again, he would stop and draw an "X" on a sign with his index finger, then continue on his way.

"I'm pretty sure he shouldn't be out unsupervised!" said Bridget.

"It's pretty odd, I'll give you that!" said Peter "I can understand the wandering but why the Peruvian poncho look?!"

"Why not?!" Bridget replied slightly defensively, her own style bordering on Goth and keen to defend people's right to wear what they wanted.

"I'm not knocking it! It suits him—but you don't see it every day!"

"He's heading across the park towards town! Cut through here Dad!" said Bridget. Peter did as instructed and pulled into the long car park that ran alongside the large field.

"That's as far as we can go" said Peter, as they watched the man casually stroll across the field towards the town centre.

"We can walk into town from here across the field" suggested Bridget.

"It's like a bog out there" said Peter concerned as he'd just cleaned the car, but Bridget had already got the door open.

"Come on Dad. It'll be frozen today!"

Not the keenest of walkers, Peter dragged himself out of the car.

"OK, get some bags from the boot then"

Bridget grabbed the bags, then looked up.

"Where's he gone?"

"Let's head that way anyway" said Peter, "perhaps we'll catch him up". They crunched their way across the frozen grass of the nearly empty park at a brisk pace but they had lost track of the Peruvian.

"We'll probably see him wandering around the shops" said Peter, pleased his shoes were staying relatively clean.

As they headed towards the stationery shop, they scanned the alleyways for the Peruvian, but he was nowhere to be seen.

"If he was here, we'd see him in that poncho!" joked Peter.

After Bridget had bought her new folder and drawing pens, she and her father shared a coffee in the café, absent-mindedly staring out at the crisp morning through the misted up front window.

"It's him!" Bridget pointed. It was definitely him, sitting near the statue.

"So it is!" said Peter "Looks like he's busking … we'll finish up here and go over". They kept an eye on him while they slurped down the last of their coffees and left the shop. The chill northerly wind found gaps in their coats as they hurried across the square towards the statue where the man was sitting.

It was definitely him, unless another busker had decided to dress up as a colourful South American, which seemed unlikely.

The music he played was in keeping with his look, an upbeat mariachi guitar style, the lively sound having drawn some people in to listen, despite the weather. All the time he played there was a broad smile across his face, black fingerless gloves keeping some of the cold from his hands.

"He's very good" said Peter, for some reason not expecting this.

"If you like that sort of thing" said Bridget.

"I do!" said Peter "Drop this into his hat"

Bridget walked over and dropped a pound coin into his hat. The Peruvian smiled and nodded as he effortlessly picked out the tune, as if the small guitar was an extension of his arms. As he played, his head frequently stretched upwards and looked to the skies.

"Mmm" said Bridget, "Not my cup of tea but he's really getting into it"

Father and daughter stayed for two more songs, not noticing the cold, fascinated by his playing style. As he ended, they and the few others clapped and he nodded thanks. Still smiling, the Peruvian picked a small flask out of an inside pocket of his poncho, unscrewed the cup and poured himself a coffee. He took a sip and warmed his hands on the cup as steam spiralled up to mix with his breath..

Peter approached him. "Thank you, that was great".

"Oh you are very kind" replied the Peruvian.

"I hope you don't mind me asking but we saw you walking into town and you seemed to be making a cross on the signs"

"Yes, that was me"

"But why?"

"It's so they know where I am"

"Who?"

"The angels" he smiled.

Peter felt he should back off at this point, conscious he was there with his daughter, but something in his eyes compelled both of them to stay.

"I am leaving today and I want them to find me"

"Where are you going?" asked Peter.

"That I do not know" replied the Peruvian "only they know, but I have a good feeling".

The signs still confused Peter.

"But you didn't leave any marks on the signs"

"They can see" he smiled "They won't be long now, I just need to wait"

Peter was still concerned. "Look if you are unwell or need somewhere to sleep we can take you somewhere".

"No, that is very kind but I am happy"

"Happy?" thought Peter, but he looked it . . . no signs of distress at all.

"OK then" smiled Peter extending his hand, "Lovely to meet you".

"Thank you" beamed the Peruvian "and may your life be long and happy!"

"And yours" Peter replied, slightly inadequately.

"What do you think Dad?" asked Bridget as they walked away "I'm worried about him. I think he needs some help"

"I think we've done all we can. He looked well enough didn't he!"

"There's a homeless shelter in town, I might give them a ring and let them know he's there"

"We don't know he's homeless though do we" said Peter.

Peter and his daughter continued their shopping and when they got home Bridget did ring the shelter. They had not heard of him but said they would keep an eye out for him over the next couple of days in their visits to the town.

For the next two days life rolled on very much as usual . . . the sun rose, the sun set and people scurried about their respective businesses.

"I wonder how our Peruvian man is?" said Peter as he browsed through the local paper watching the TV.

"I was thinking of going into town tomorrow so I'll have a look out for him" .

Then something caught Bridget's eye . . .

"Dad" she said dead-pan, her eyes fixed to what she had seen on the back of her Dad's paper

"Busker found dead in town centre"

Peter turned over the page and started to read. "Oh no".

"...his body was found by the statue wrapped in a coloured blanket ... on 13th January"

"It was the night after we left him" said Bridget "I knew we should have got him some help. He probably froze to death!"

"We couldn't force it on him" said Peter. Both of them couldn't help feeling a sadness, like they'd lost someone they knew much better than they had.

"It's silly" said Bridget clearing a moist eye "we only knew him for ten minutes ..."

The following morning the weather hadn't improved much. Snow started to fall from the light grey sky but at least the biting wind had calmed to a breeze.

Half asleep, Bridget opened the front door to fetch the milk from the step. The milk had frozen and pushed the foil cap off the glass bottle ... and tucked behind the plant pot, sheltered from the snow under the porch, was a small guitar.

Plastic Man

June had always thought there was something magical about her island, an atmosphere that was hard to put her finger on. And she *did* think of it as "her" island, even though it was Sam's. She wished it *was* hers but just knowing the owner and having the opportunity to visit was enough for her. Sitting on the porch of the colonial-style Mauritian beach house overlooking the large lawn, it occurred to her that things could be worse … she could be back in her flat in Bermonsdsey in the light drizzle instead of contemplating a barefoot walk across the lawn, through the palms and onto the private beach on "her" private island. June had been there two days and preparations for Sam's 35th birthday party were progressing well. It was a minor miracle she was there at all after her years of working for Sam as his PA. Gregarious, confident, blustering, intensely annoying, charming … these are all terms she would use to describe him, qualities that no doubt helped him achieve great success in his packaging business. The "intensely annoying" wasn't an exaggeration but there was something about him she couldn't help but like, despite his efforts to frustrate … an honesty and a directness that kept her from looking for alternative employment … and Sam had always looked after her. Over the years, he would have liked her to be a more "personal" assistant despite their thirteen year age gap, not that anyone would have guessed that, Sam's hard living adding years to his appearance and June looking considerably younger than her 48. She had enjoyed a few shorter relationships but had been living on her own for some years now. She knew Sam wasn't one to settle and so had avoided that particular complication, despite much persistence on Sam's part. Anyway, she felt more like his mother most of the time, making sure he was where he was supposed to be on time and generally clearing up after him.

June walked barefoot between the vibrant orange and blue flower beds on the lawn, through the palms, out onto the bright white sand, and sighed heavily at the view. The results of Sam's old business was irritating her, and not for the first time. She had only just cleared some flotsam and jetsam from the beach yesterday but each tide seemed to bring a little more in. The odd lobster pot and buoy was quite decorative but it was the plastic bottles, drinks cartons, milk containers, oil cans, margarine tubs, pens, the variety was endless. It wasn't a lot but any litter offended her compulsive tidiness so she made a call for the beach to be cleared again. It was the day of Sam's party and she wanted everything to look as good as it possibly could. The decoration of the house and grounds had been largely organised from London, along with all the caterers and servers, so today was really just tying up loose ends and making sure what she had planned actually happened. She wasn't unduly worried as it wasn't the first time she'd organised a party for him.

"June, I need you!" the conversation had gone.

"Oh yes?" June joked "What about that twenty-five year old girlfriend?"

"Yeah, she's lovely but she couldn't organise her way out of a wet paper bag! And you know your way around out here . . . please June, you'll love it and you won't have to spend a penny!"

It did appeal to her, but she didn't want Sam to know.

"Go on then, you've twisted my arm!"

"Fabulous! It'll be like the old days!"

"Oh no!" smiled June "Me frantically trying to keep you out of the papers?"

"Are you suggesting I could be a little indiscreet?!" joked Sam.

"It has been known" replied June.

The house looked spectacular. People still talked about the parties in the 90's that June had organised in London. Of course the scale of the tropical setting helped but somehow June instinctively knew how to choreograph a spectacular, magical event. The sheets of twinkling lights draped across walls, the uplighting of the palms and pillars, the immaculately formal staff, efficient yet friendly, the string quartet, the jazz ensemble . . . the word was indeed "magical", an atmosphere of reality being suspended. And the weather had been kind, part of June's planning but there was always an element of good fortune. This evening, the lightest of breezes gently swayed the palm fronds and cooled brows, but never intruded. Guests started to arrive, some that June remembered from the old days who were genuinely pleased to see her:

"I don't know how you put up with him June"

"You haven't changed a bit!"

"I tell you, he wouldn't be here now without you!"

She was pleased that the party plan was coming together, with a good-humoured, easy-going atmosphere developing, the most difficult thing to plan.

"June!" Sam called from the bar. He ordered another Martini for her and walked across smiling.

"You've done it again!"

"Yes it seems to be going well doesn't it".

"It's perfect!" replied Sam, full of admiration.

June knew that this was perhaps not the best time to mention the litter on the beach but she couldn't help herself.

"Have you noticed the plastic down on the beach lately?"

"Mmm" said Sam sipping his Martini, "not really if I'm honest" he replied.

"I don't want to go on about it but they say it's most days now"

"It's a small price to pay for the progress" said Sam tongue-in-cheek, waiting for a reaction.

"Small price! You don't have to clear it up!"

"True enough" said Sam sipping some more.

"And what about the birds?" said June.

"What birds? I like the birds!"

"Jodie said she found a dead cormorant wrapped in one of those nylon box bands the other day. I think it's appalling" snapped June.

"Of course, nobody wants that" agreed Sam "but I *could* say look at all the benefits that plastics have brought everybody". He knew he was pushing it pursuing this line of argument.

"Yes but, it's all the plastic packaging isn't it!" said June directly attacking the business she helped him to build up and feeling that she had contributed to the problem.

"You've got to put oil and fizzy drinks in *something*!" said Sam "a paper bag won't hold them for long!"

"You know there's alternatives!" said June, "That hemp stuff that biodegrades, . . . I heard someone say that in fifty days it's gone. That's got to be better hasn't it?"

"Yes, yes, I know, but the old-school companies have got to make their money too! *We wouldn't be here if I hadn't!*" He was correctly pointing out that the only reason he owned an island was the proceeds of the sale of his plastic injection moulding company.

"You're a wealthy man Sam!" said June sternly "You have a duty to make amends in some way for what you have contributed to"

"It's all getting a bit serious isn't it!" laughed Sam, "Let's get you another Martini!"

"By the way" said Sam changing the subject "I have never seen *anything* like that cake!" The birthday cake was spectacular and had even taken June aback when she had first seen it. She had a vison of what it might look like, but it exceeded even her high expectations . . . a blue tinted multi-layered dripping cascade, flanked by thin, irregular sheets of ice like the entrance to a glacial cave just starting to thaw, the ice perfectly clear and perforated with holes. A tinkling glass announced that it was nine o'clock and time for Sam to cut the cake. People started to gather and Sam was handed a knife.

"Speech!" someone shouted.

"OK, OK!" smiled Sam, the several Martinis now starting to take their toll.

"Thirty-five! Who'd have thought I'd make it to this grand old age!" he said in jest. "Thank you everybody for coming and making tonight so special for me. Tonight I have only invited people I really want to be with". People laughed.

"No really" Sam said seriously "You know some parties you invite people because you think you should . . . well this isn't one of those. You all mean a lot to me and I want to thank you for your support and friendship"

"And cash!" shouted Chris from the back, a major investor in the past.

"Ha! Yes, and your cash Chris!"

He held the knife, looked up to the stars on this perfect evening and finished his Martini.

"Make a wish you old bastard" rose up from the back.

"You only get one, mind!" People laughed...

The Martinis mustered a reply for him as he raised his glass unsteadily.

"I wish... I wish all the bloody plastic around here would *sink*...yes, I wish all the plastic would *sink and not float* and perhaps it wouldn't be in the news so bloody often!" People roared with laughter, all except June who was smiling but shaking her head.

As the commotion died down, Sam walked over to June and took her arm.

"Bloody fantastic cake!" he said, voice slightly slurred.

"It really was wasn't it!" she agreed as they turned to walk out onto the old jetty, raised above the moonlit water.

"You're right" he said decisively.

"About what? The cake?"

"No not the cake!" he dismissed "*about making amends*. You're right".

"Oh" she replied quite surprised.

"I've still got contacts in the business and I *will* make amends!" he shouted spinning around on the jetty.

"OK. That's good!" June smiled.

"*I will make amends, I promise you!*" he shouted as he whirled round on the jetty.

June laughed out loud "Be careful Sam!"

They laughed as the moonlight danced on the sea and the jazz ensemble played on the lawn. Sam stopped sharply and turned towards her.

"June" he announced. As he turned, his heel slipped on some algae on the wooden decking, something he'd been meaning to get cleaned for ages (something June wouldn't have allowed to accumulate) and he fell backwards off the jetty.

"Sam!" June shouted as she rushed to the edge.

When he first surfaced Sam laughed, the soaking sobering him up a little but the weight of his jacket started to pull him down.

"It's OK June!" he spluttered.

"Take your jacket off" she shouted.

"I'm treading water June!" he laughed. She ran towards the orange lifebelt hung on a post nearby. Seeing he was having trouble now, she held the end of the rope and hurled it towards him. As the plastic lifebelt hit the water, it sank like a stone right next to him, dragging the rope down with it. Sam had gotten his wish . . . and it couldn't have been more inconvenient . . .

"June!" Sam spluttered, no longer laughing, now having genuine trouble untangling himself from his jacket. Without thinking June jumped in. The water was warm and her light clothes made it easy to swim. Her school life-saving techniques seemed to rush back to her as she calmly supported his chin and pulled him into some steps. They slowly hauled themselves up the steps and Sam slumped on his back on the jetty. June crouched down beside him . . . he was breathing and had a good colour. She sat back with huge relief.

Sam turned over and reached out his arm to her.

"Stay with me June". There was a desperation in his eyes that told her he really meant it.

"I need you June. Stay with me" said Sam holding tightly onto her hand with both of his.

"It's the Martini speaking" she said.

"No, it isn't"

It took her some time but June did eventually decide to stay with Sam. And he did start to make amends . . .

June had always thought there was something magical about her island, an atmosphere that was hard to put her finger on.

Animal Magnetism

"What am I going to do for four days on a *narrow boat*?!" shouted ten year old Lee. His Dad had already booked the holiday in an impetuous moment thinking that it might be a bit of an adventure for them.

"There's loads to do, don't you worry, I'll even let you have a go at steering the boat"

"*Really?*" said Lee doubtfully.

"Yes *really*, you can actually drive the thing for some of the time"

"Does it have Wi-Fi?"

"I'm sure it does" assured Tony his father.

"It *doesn't* have Wi-Fi does it!"

"It's everywhere these days isn't it, so it's bound to have it" said Tony, thinking he had better check. Perhaps he had been a bit hasty booking it, but he needed something to do with him while his wife was away for work.

"Look, it'll be a break, and it's only a few days"

"A few days!" Lee shouted "What am I going to do?!"

Tony had thought this might be his reaction and he had not yet played his trump card . . . and this was the time to deploy it.

"What do you think of that then!" announced Tony proudly as he placed a heavy metal ring on the table.

"What the hell is that?!"

"It's a very powerful magnet. Look."

Lifting it like a heavy knuckle duster, Tony moved the magnet close to a fork and spoon laying on a china plate on the kitchen table. With the magnet half a metre away, the cutlery flew off the plate and stuck to the magnet with a ping!

"Woooah!" said Lee, 100% of his attention gripped. Tony smiled. It had worked like a charm.

"Now, here's the plan … We're going to attach a strong line to this baby and trawl it behind us on the boat and see what we can catch!"

"Mmmm …" said Lee reluctant to sound too enthusiastic.

"Think about it, there's going to be a ton of stuff at the bottom of the canal, all sorts of treasure that people have dropped over the side!. And if there's anything metal, this baby is going to pick it up. Here, you have a go!" said Tony passing the magnet. "Try that bowl on the shelf there".

Lee approached the shelf, a little in awe of the power of the magnet.

"Little bit closer" smiled Tony.

"It moved!" shouted Lee.

"Tiny bit more" said Tony. And the bowl shot off the shelf and clanged onto the magnet.

"Ha! That's amazing!" Father and son laughed together and Tony knew he'd rescued the trip.

"I still want Wi-Fi though" smiled Lee.

On the morning of the trip, Lee was actually quite excited. He'd been playing with the magnet for the last couple of days and despite his Dad warning him to keep it away from anything electrical, a laptop was playing up and the radio in the kitchen didn't sound like it should. One thing that had really swung it for him was the reaction of his friends … they couldn't get enough of it and Lee had assumed almost super hero status with his new magnetic powers.

"Have you packed enough clothes?" Tony asked his son, guilty that he hadn't personally checked.

"Yeah, should be fine" Although he was only ten, Lee could normally be relied on for such things.

"OK, last chance!" smiled Tony as he shut the boot of the car.

As they unloaded into the canal boat, the sun came out, with just a cool breeze drifting off the water. Absolutely perfect.

"It's a lot bigger than I thought" smiled Lee.

"This was a small one" laughed Tony as he boarded "They do them *twice* this length! Maybe we'll get one of those with your Mum if you like it"

Lee *did* like it.

"Look!" said Tony in a muted shout "A heron!"

"Wow, it's huge!" said Lee, more used to the sparrows and blackbirds in town. His Dad chugged the boat down the tree-lined canal looking forward to slowing down a little and spending some time with his son.

"Is this as fast as it goes?!" said Lee.

" 'Fraid so, can you guess how fast?"

Lee knew the speed limit outside his school.

"Twenty miles an hour?"

"Lower" said his Dad.

"Ten?"

"Lower!"

"Three?"

"No, it's not that slow!" laughed Tony, "Four miles an hour! And that's flat out!"

They both chuckled but neither of them were bothered by the lack of speed.

Tony negotiated some bends in the river and was getting the feel of the boat.

The girl that had taken them through the basic controls said that the secret was to take things slowly and remember the boat takes a little time to respond to the tiller, and to slow down. It was as if the boat was forcing them to slow down to the pace of river life. And they both soon did . . . at times they were quite close to parts of the town but with the trees and the fact that they were sitting low in the canal, they never knew it. It all felt a million miles away.

"Look Dad!" Lee pointed, as a vole swam frantically across the river, his nose breaking the water like the bow of the boat.

"Ha!" laughed Tony "he'd better watch out for us learner drivers" as he steered the boat gently round the animal.

"Can I have a go Dad?"

"Sure. Hop over here then". Lee had expected a "no" as they'd only been on the water an hour or so.

"Hold onto the tiller here" said Tony "This steers the boat". Tony eased Lee's hand to the left and the boat started to turn right.

"Cool!" said Lee.

"And the other way turns it back . . . but it takes a little while"

To Tony's surprise, Lee took to it like a duck to water.

"And how do I slow it down?"

"You want to go *slower*?!" asked Tony, surprised.

"Yeah, how?"

"This small lever here, just ease it back a little . . . and you can hear the engine slowing down"

"And push it forwards gently to speed up again, but look out for that bridge coming up!"

"I'm OK Dad"

"Well, Lets do it together shall we" suggested Tony, placing guiding hands on the controls. Lee was happy with that as they drifted gracefully under the low brick arch of the bridge.

"Shout for an echo!" said Tony, regressing to his childhood.

"Ahhhhhh" laughed Lee. Against all the odds, the trip was working out just fine.

Tony hadn't mentioned the locks to Lee, but he absolutely loved them. It was fortunate Lee was fairly big for his age as he just about had the strength to move the heavy gates as his Dad negotiated the boat in and out, being careful not to hit the sides. Lee was now quite impressed with his Dad's boatmanship

"Not bad Dad!" he shouted as he jumped back on board.

"Not bad yourself!" replied Tony "Well done!"

They had both soon slowed down to river pace, the birds, the locks, the other boats taking up so much of their attention that they'd almost forgotten . . .

"The magnet!" shouted Lee, "Can I have a go now?" he asked.

"Ah yes!" laughed Tony "We'll pull up over here and get a line on it now."

After pulling the boat to the side of the canal and shutting the engine down, Tony sorted out the line that he'd bought for the magnet.

"There, that should do it" There was about ten metres of light rope.

"If we tie the end onto the boat it we won't lose it if you drop the rope" suggested Tony.

"Good thinking" replied Lee, conceding that his Dad did occasionally talk some sense. With the end of the rope tied to the mooring point at the back of the boat, they pulled away.

"Throw it in then!" shouted Tony. It plopped loudly into the water and immediately sank to the bottom, trawling nicely as Tony had planned.

"We'll drag it along for a while and see what we get!" said Tony from the tiller.

After two minutes, Lee couldn't wait any longer . . . "I'm pulling it in Dad!"

Eagerly hauling the heavy magnet back to the boat, as soon as it was out of the water he could see he had something . . .

"We've got something!" Lee shouted, swinging the magnet up on deck.

Tony laughed out loud "Well I won't be retiring just yet!" as, with some difficulty, Lee prised a rusty old bean tin off the magnet.

"Oo look on the back too!" pointed his Dad . . . a bolt and two screws were firmly attached. It didn't seem to bother Lee what was on the magnet, he was just happy he'd caught something. He carefully put the bolts into the corroded can and threw the magnet back in.

"Fingers crossed!" smiled Tony, pleased that his son had forgotten about the WiFi.

The rest of the day, Lee was on a mission . . . his sole focus was to trawl with the magnet and there were rich pickings from the canal bottom: more tins, bolts, scaffold fittings, a child's seat off a shopping trolley, a circular chromed ladies powder compact and two pens (one that actually looked quite good). Tony was feeling a little bad that he hadn't pointed out that precious metals weren't magnetic, but he saw no reason to spoil Lee's fun with that knowledge. They dragged up the remains of a child's scooter but Tony talked Lee into throwing that one back . . . they even unearthed a whole shopping trolley but the weeds won in the tug of war between them and the magnet.

That evening, as father and son ate some sandwiches on deck, Tony perused his son's treasures. Lee had added a spam can, a tent peg and some colourful fishing tackle. He tried to get the lid off the circular ladies powder compact but despite trying to get his nails in the gap, it wouldn't budge. He liked the look of the more expensive looking Parker pen and tried it on the newspaper, but it promptly tore the front page.

"We'll have another go tomorrow" said Tony, as his son gathered his haul and placed it in a cardboard box. It had been an eventful day and they had both tired a lot earlier than usual.

"Thanks for the trip Dad" said Lee "It's been great today". "That's all right" replied Tony surprised and delighted. "Get some rest now and we'll see what we can catch tomorrow." They hugged and Lee headed off to bed.

Just before Lee settled down to sleep, he laid out his treasures on the shelf by the window next to his bed. He could overhear his Dad talking to his Mum over the phone, checking that all was well with her. It seemed to be, so feeling tired and content, he settled down to sleep, the gentle rocking of the boat on the water soon sending him off.

Two hours later, a full moon streaming silver light onto Tony's bed, the compact had dried out enough and it quietly clicked open in the centre. A bright white light shone in all directions from the crack as the lid slowly continued to rise, not from a hinge at the back but straight upwards on five small posts. As it stopped opening, a small ramp illuminated in soft blue extended to meet the shelf . . . and out stepped the spiders from Mars. Their landing in the river wasn't planned and although the ship hadn't let in any water, several systems were not fully operational. But now, out of the water and a little drier, things were much better . . .

Seven tiny spiders crawled down the ramp and into the boat that night. Now at last, they could begin what they had come here to do.